CHAPTER ONE

CELIA KINGSLEY replaced the telephone receiver carefully and stood staring at it for several long seconds before turning to transfer her dark blue gaze to her aunt, who sat apparently oblivious by the fire, idly pursuing the evening paper. The firelight, flickering over her, reflected her cosily in the old silver teapot which stood on the low table by her side, where two half empty cups of tea were rapidly growing cold. A normal scene on a rather chilly December afternoon. Or, thought Celia with sudden exasperation, it had been until the telephone rang. She could feel a familiar, painful tension mounting inside her, drawing her nerves as taut as violin strings.

'I do so appreciate a fire at this time of year,' Mary Martin murmured, deliberately trite in her effort to avoid the implications of Celia's frowning face. She was quite aware that Celia had been speaking to her brother in Manchester and was not at all keen to hear the missing side of that conversation. Celia's tone of voice had actually told her all she wished to know!

Yet, when Celia did eventually speak, she was startled. 'That was Robin,' she explained unnecessarily. 'He would like me to go home for Christmas. Lucy is in some kind of trouble.'

'Oh, dear!' For one apprehensive moment Mary's pleasant face went blank. 'It surely can't be anything serious?'

'No, no, of course not. At least ...' Celia's sensitively curved mouth twisted impatiently, and the small frown between her smooth brows grew more obvious as she hesitated. Why couldn't Robin lose the habit of consulting her every time he had a problem? He never contacted her other-

5

wise, and although his problems were usually domestic this one didn't seem to come into this category. Now, because of the unfortunate phrasing of a sentence, she had aroused Mary's curiosity and must find a suitable explanation, but there were some people she hated having to mention, no matter what the circumstances!

At last she continued, forcing the words from her reluctant lips. 'I believe she's become involved with a man. Did you ever know a Denis Ryland? He happens to be Guy Ryland's cousin and Robin isn't at all sure what to do about it.'

'I see.' Clearly unable to, Mary Martin pondered. 'No, I don't seem to remember any Denis Ryland, although of course I know of Guy. But if Lucy is friendly with this man, why should Robin feel he has to do something about it? Does he mean that Guy doesn't approve?'

'No.' Really, when Mary chose she could be deliberately obtuse. 'According to Robin, Guy Ryland doesn't know about it yet and, being Robin, he hasn't the faintest idea how to handle the situation!'

'But surely, dear . . .'

Still seething with annoyance, Celia cut through Mary's tentative sentence with another impatient sigh. Turning sharply she flopped down in the nearest chair. Too well she could read what was on her aunt's mind. Why shouldn't Lucy, at twenty-one, be allowed to have a romance with whoever she liked, even if it had to be one of the hated Rylands? It couldn't matter that both Lucy and Robin worked for the firm. Aunt Mary just didn't understand, nor could she probably be expected to.

Restraining a sudden desire to throw something, Celia apologised automatically for her ill-temper, attempting wryly some sort of explanation. 'Guy Ryland, Robin thinks, has plans for Denis which don't include Lucy, and Robin is too fond of his present position to want to jeopardise it in any way. Hence the panic!'

'Ah.' A little wiser, Mary raised her eyebrows. 'And he

would like you to go and talk to her, no doubt? Well, dear, looking at it entirely from a man's point of view, that should solve everything. How does one talk to a girl in love?'

'I wouldn't know.'

Subconsciously aware in Celia's voice of a certain reserve, Mary glanced at her swiftly. 'It's not as if you have much personal experience to draw on. I really think Robin is asking too much.'

From anyone else but Mary this direct reference to her own comparatively uncomplicated life might have hurt, but Mary, Celia acknowledged, was much too nice a person to indulge lightly in this sort of sarcasm.

She was proved right when Mary, after a slight pause, added hastily, 'You know I didn't mean that unkindly. You've always been too busy.'

'I suppose I was once.' Bemused, because she hadn't thought about it for a long time, Celia stared rather blindly into the fire. 'Not now, though. Not since I came to London.'

'Well, you do have your job, and lately your modelling agency has been quite demanding.'

'If a little advertising for toothpaste and bath-salts for television commercials could be so called,' Celia shrugged her slim shoulders indifferently. 'It's not really my thing, although I admit it's helped financially, but what wouldn't I give to be doing something I really enjoyed!'

Rather bitterly her thoughts swung back to Manchester, to the shop, to the days when her father had been alive and owned it. Life then, before the Rylands had taken over, had been hectic but fun. She had devoted all her intelligence and strength to learning the family business and hadn't minded that there had been little time left over for romance. Besides, she mused wryly, romance wasn't something one could purchase over a counter, and she'd never met any man yet who had attracted her greatly.

Always she had found herself totally preoccupied with the store. Robin, although older, had barely been interested,

7

showing no particular keenness to become—in his own words—a shopkeeper. That he had changed a lot since then only seemed to add to her regrets. Hastily Celia concentrated on her sister, and assured her aunt, 'The situation is perhaps not so desperate as Robin tries to make out. Lucy probably only needs someone to confide in.'

'I don't wonder,' Celia's tone was emphatic, 'there can't be much fun for a girl in a place like Manchester.'

Celia felt a quick twinge of indignation. 'There's not all that much wrong with Manchester!' she heard herself proclaiming impulsively, while wondering why she should be so automatically loyal. She had been born there, of course, but never considered she had any special love for it.

'Manchester,' Mary retorted, unimpressed, 'is fine when viewed from a distance. You were fortunate to escape, even considering the circumstances. The greatest disasters often conceal a blessing or two. It's just a pity Lucy didn't come with you, but then someone had to stay behind to look after the house, I suppose.'

Did she detect another note of censure? Celia flicked Mary a bewildered glance. Lucy was two years younger than herself and had been Mary's favourite when they were children. 'I know I should have stayed,' she confessed, 'but after the crash—well, you know how it was, I just couldn't. When Daddy lost everything I felt a terrible sense of responsibility. I've always felt I ought to have seen it coming!'

Mary looked at her quickly, really startled by this. It was the first time the girl had actually admitted so much, and it was all so ridiculous. Dismay smote her, causing her to speak more sharply than she intended. 'The crash was unavoidable, my dear. I'd seen it coming almost since your mother died, when you were still at school. Part of your father died with her—we all knew that. He lost the necessary drive to contend with the competition in big business today. Younger and more energetic men than your father have gone down; I don't think you can reproach yourself in

8

any way. You were always an enormous help to him, but you were really too young.'

'Oh, come off it, Mary.' Bleakly ironical, Celia tossed back her long tawny hair. 'It was only three years ago. I was twenty and learning fast. I had ability—look how well I've done in London.'

Celia's voice was low, but the bitterness wedged in her soft tones was unmistakable. Mary sighed. Celia had never been so forthcoming before, and while she didn't doubt it might be a good thing even at this late stage to discuss it openly, there were many small details concerning her brother-in-law's near-bankruptcy which Mary had almost completely forgotten. Because Celia had appeared to settle down in London very quickly, Mary had concluded that the subsequent disposal of the large Kingsley Department Store hadn't affected Celia so very deeply. Not a little shocked, she saw now that it was still there, the strain in the tightly clenched fingers, the unhappy shadows around her wide blue eyes. Celia was a beautiful girl, but apart from this she was too sweet to be allowed to live with something like this on her mind for the rest of her life.

'You know, darling,' Mary spoke to her gently, 'that things had gone too far. Your father told me so himself. If Guy Ryland hadn't stepped in when he did it could all have been much worse.'

'Guy Ryland never did anything for nothing!'

'No, dear, I'm not suggesting he would, but you must admit he showed more generosity than others might have done in the circumstances.'

'I'm sorry, Mary, I can't really agree,' Celia replied flatly, not willing to change her long standing opinion. He was their enemy, that one! Fiercely she clutched the conviction to her. Robin and Lucy, because they continued to work for him, had, she considered, betrayed their family pride. How Guy Ryland must have laughed when they had both willingly agreed to stay on under new management, letting themselves be manipulated like puppets on a string!

It had been something which had made her doubly determined never to return—that, and the memory of that last dreadful scene, an incident for which she held Guy directly responsible. It had been dreadful because he had provoked her into doing something she had never done before or since. She had actually hit a man, and the dreadful thing was that the violence was still there within her, not seemingly in any way diminished by the passing years. No matter how she tried she could not completely forget, and the tenacious strength of this emotion seemed, in some peculiar sort of way, to preclude the possiblity of any gentler one ever entering her heart.

It was crazily unexplainable that whenever she was introduced to a man Guy Ryland seemed to come between them, like a recurring evil wished on her by a malicious fate. Instead of an interesting new face she saw only his—his as she had seen it that last evening at home, after she had slapped it with all her strength, with all the pent-up fury of her own inescapable unhappiness.

Even now when she thought about it she shuddered, still able to feel the cold contact of his hard cheek. Late at night he had come to the house to see her father. She had not had any warning of his visit and had reluctantly explained how her father was exhausted and had been forced to retire early to bed. Robin and Lucy had both been out.

Guy Ryland had not, as Celia expected, accepted this and gone away. Instead he had pushed almost forcibly past her into the hall, obviously with little sympathy for her dithering apprehension. 'You might do instead,' he'd said abruptly, having no comment apparently to spare for her weary parent.

Clearly still Celia remembered her own angry surprise as unwillingly she had closed the door. She had remained beside it, giving, she had hoped, an unmistakable indication that he wasn't welcome and that his visit could only be of a very short duration.

Never before had she seen him this close. Always, since

10

she had first learnt he was taking over the store, she had deliberately avoided him. Her curiosity, tantalised for weeks by only brief glimpses, seemed to leap forward on its own volition.

In front of her she had seen a man in his thirties, a man with the calculating reckless expression of one who knows exactly where he is going. His good looks were brilliant, of a kind not easily forgotten, entangled as his were with every inch of his personality. There had been about him a certain inflexibility, an aggressiveness to his mouth that suggested he was a man used to getting his own way. Strategically he might use some veneer of sophistication to conceal it, but intuitively Celia felt her summing up to be correct. Inwardly, as she had stood staring up at him, she had shuddered with a growing dislike, and when her prolonged silence had succeeded in raising his pugnacious eyebrows she had cried coldly, 'I don't think I would be willing to help you, Mr Ryland, even if I could!'

It had been a bald statement, not uttered with the intention of doing anything else but displease. A brief declaration of non-cooperation; an unmistakable declaration of war! It had all been there in the wintry bleakness of her eyes, the clear sharpness of her voice as she had continued to hold his dark glance. Behind her short, terse sentence lay a world of unspoken disapproval which a less astute man than Guy Ryland wouldn't have found difficult to sense.

That he took exception to it had been immediately apparent. It had been there in the swift thinning of his mouth, his almost audible indrawn breath. 'And so,' he had exclaimed coolly, 'we have here the clever Celia—unless I'm mistaken?'

An underlying contempt in his tones had told her instinctively that he was annoyed by his unfriendly reception and could give as good as was sent. Crossing words with a mere girl would be beneath him, although he wouldn't demean himself by saying so outright. Yet had he ex-

11

pected, she had wondered wildly, that she should fall into his arms, hailing him as a hero, the man who had literally stolen their store! The sarcasm in his voice as he had mentioned her name had added immeasurably to her fury.

'The downfall of the shop was in no way my fault,' she had snapped, childishly angry.

'Does it have to be anyone's particular fault?' His eyes, narrowly appraising, had held an element of controlled insolence.

An insolence that had aroused an almost unknown lack of civility in herself. 'Don't insult me with platitudes,' she had choked, bright colour surging in her smooth young cheeks. 'The victor never has anything less for the vanquished than contempt!'

'Oh, come now, Celia——' this time his voice had been edged with a dry impatience, a determination, in spite of provocation, to exercise a little restraint. 'Beneath your father's management,' he went on after a slight hesitation, 'the firm went down. Someone had to take over. It would be extremely foolish to blame a mere girl like yourself for what happened. You can't have been long out of the school-room, surely?'

'Long enough.' His reference to her apparent immaturity had only heaped coals on the fire. Far from being appeased by his thread of tolerance, tears had stung her eye-lids hotly and in an attempt to disguise them she had heard herself almost shouting, 'I do happen to know what's been going on!'

'Ah, yes, I was forgetting!' Obviously controlling his own rising temper, he allowed a glint of sardonic amusement. 'You're supposed to work at the store, I believe, even if during the past few days you've been conspicuous by your absence—not the sort of example I like set for the rest of my staff. It might be a good idea if I saw you personally tomorrow. You clearly need to be straightened out.'

Celia had stared at him, positively glared at him. The thought of entering those huge premises, traversing all the many different departments as a mere employee, had proved too great a strain on her pride, that trait within her which Robin and Lucy possessed only to a far lesser degree. With them it wasn't all-consuming as it had been with her, but she doubted if anyone had guessed. She hadn't flaunted it, being almost unaware it was there. Only Guy Ryland had seen it in the uplifted tilt of her delicate chin, the haughty angle of her small head. He had guessed, and she had known he had, and she had hated him for it!

Loudly defiant, she had proclaimed, 'I'll never enter the shop again. Not while it's in the hands of a scoundrel like you, a man whose sole aim in life appears to be the ruination of others. You've had your eye on our shop—the site, for years. You can't deny it!'

'Why, you little devil!' The anger was back, pounding in his voice as he grabbed the wrist which Celia had flung up to hide her tears but obviously had seemed raised to hit him.

The idea had not occurred to her until that moment, until his fingers cracked like steel around the slender bone. Then it had been that her free hand, driven by a half frightened fury at the peculiar feeling which whipped through her at his touch, had shot out defensively, making unerring contact with his cheek.

It was something she recalled as clearly as if it had only just happened. For one frozen moment there had been absolute silence and she had stared helplessly at the spreading red marks on the smoothly shaven skin. She still remembered the texture of it. It had felt hard, as remarkably vital as the man himself, and, as her eyes clung, there had been the completely devastating notion that she had made a dreadful mistake.

Aghast, as she stared, she had been aware of the ruthless line of his mouth and in his eyes a glinting, wholly unforgiving coldness which held her momentarily paralysed. As if she had struck herself she had been aware of pain, of a sensation she couldn't understand sweeping her entire body,

13

so intense as to render her incapable of moving. And, before she could sufficiently recover her senses, her other arm had been clipped in a vice-like grip which had jerked her rudely to him. His face had suddenly been too close, the near-visual effect of hard masculine aggression almost too much for her. Before she could prevent it an alarmed gasp had escaped her quivering lips. But being the man he was he had taken no notice.

'No one,' he'd informed her grimly, with cool emphasis, 'ever hits me! Others,' he assured her, 'have tried something less and failed. You're going to live to regret what you've done tonight, my dear Celia, if you did but know it.'

His voice had been expressionless. She had been completely locked in a sort of curious dread that he would begin to extract some terrible revenge. Frantically she had begun to pull away from him. 'Let me go!' she cried, and her voice, reflecting some of her inner turmoil, sounded wild even to her own ears.

But for a few more punishing seconds Guy Ryland had continued to hold her, his glance scorching over her, his eyes seemingly able to transfix her wholly. The air seemed suddenly static, like the lull before the storm, and when he spoke his words brought little comfort. 'Oh, yes, Miss Kingsley,' he had said, I intend letting you go, so don't worry. But only for a little while, so I shouldn't advise you to be too complacent. Some forms of chastisement take time, and you will no doubt understand that this is something I'm short of at the moment, but I do have patience. I can wait.'

He had been quite brutal, his voice silky, licking like wildlife along her veins. 'You can't threaten me,' she had whispered vehemently, her throat restricted, her whole being caught in a whirlpool encompassed by a pair of glinting dark eyes. Scornfully now she recalled her mounting terror, her swift, irrational fear of something beyond her experience—something which her relatively sheltered life had in no way prepared her for.

14

Her heart pounding, she had heard his brief laughter, as if her shivery, tormented state provided a kind of abject amusement. 'I never waste time on threats, Miss Kingsley,' he had retorted, 'I always deal in facts. My reprisal when it comes will be quite something, a lesson which I think you might remember for a long time. I merely mentioned a slight postponement. In the meantime, as you feel unable to help me with my queries, I shall see you tomorrow, my dear.'

He released her so abruptly that she had experienced a strange sense of vertigo. Unforgivingly relentless, he had flung her hands back to her sides and strode through the door. Once she was free of him her courage had returned, but the implications of his words stayed with her, holding her rigid where she was standing, careless of the cold.

He was a new, frightening dimension, quite incomprehensible, and her heart had quivered with shock, but there was one thing she had recognised. If she was guilty of a false pride Guy Ryland had more than enough himself to match her own, but unlike hers, his had remained relatively unscathed. In recent weeks while her own conceit might have taken a few knocks, until she had slapped him his had never even been dented!

Next day Celia hadn't seen him. Soon after lunch she had been on her way to London, to the comparative safety of Aunt Mary, although she hadn't allowed herself to think of it like that. She hadn't intended, even before meeting Guy Ryland, to go back to the shop, having convinced herself that she could never work under anyone who sat at her father's desk; but until that dreadful evening when she had actually met Guy Ryland she had made no alternative plans. Now, for the first time, she acknowledged that a sudden irrational fear of the man had been almost wholly responsible for her ridiculous flight from Manchester.

Yet what else could she have done? Whatever Guy Ryland's intentions, if indeed he had had any at all, she had no means of knowing just how far he would go. With her lack of experience how could she have risked the possibility that he wouldn't forget? Some inviolate part of her had refused to consider being literally taken over, being punished in an exaggerated fashion for what after all had not been so very great a crime.

Lucy, not a little envious, had stayed at home. She had left school a year ago and worked at the store. Celia had hated leaving her, but there had been her father and Robin. There had been also Mrs Timpson who had kept house for them since their mother died, and who had assured Celia in the nicest possible way that if she really wanted to go they could manage without her.

Her father, although depressed, had not been ill. If he had been Celia would have stayed, but her departure had actually seemed to please him a little and he had agreed that until everything settled down a change might do her good. His seeming indifference to the fate of his shop had never ceased to astonish her, and made her leaving easier than it might otherwise have been. Nonetheless, she had known heartbreaking regret when he had died quite suddenly only a few weeks later.

'I don't think your going away had anything to do with it,' Timmy, as they affectionately called Mrs Timpson, had said when Celia returned briefly for the funeral. 'He understood how you felt about the store. He had Lucy and Robin, but it was your mother he needed at this particular time.'

Celia had stayed no longer than necessary. There had been very little to attend to. There had been no money— only the house, which had been left to Robin, where he and Lucy continued to live. She had seen nothing of Guy Ryland at all.

With a guilty start she realised Mary was talking and she hadn't heard a word. 'I'm sorry,' she said, slightly shamefaced, 'I'm afraid I wasn't listening.'

'Obviously not!' Mary retorted sharply. 'I was merely

pointing out that Guy Ryland did allow your father to stay on at the shop.'

'Only until he was of no more use to him.'

'Your father wanted to retire, dear, even before the crash. He often talked of it. I don't think anyone forced him.'

'Really, Aunt Mary!' Indignant, Celia straightened abruptly in her chair. 'You're almost as gullible as they are at home. You all like to imagine there's an element of humanity in Guy Ryland—in big business, but we all know that Rylands were too big to allow for this long before they took over our premises. Our collapse did nothing to soften them up or make them suddenly realise the error of their ways.'

'The error, I should imagine, lies more in the pattern of things today,' Mary commented dryly. 'Commercially, it seems, one must either get big and stay big or get out.'

Stubbornly Celia shook her head. 'There must still be a place for the man with less ambition. I hate expansion when it produces dictators like Guy Ryland.'

Mary frowned. 'You're probably being unfair. I'm sure expansion in the right way can do nothing but good. The wonder is that your father failed to see it.'

'He might have done,' Celia admitted reluctantly. 'Occasionally I remember he talked about it vaguely, but probably he didn't have the energy or incentive to do much about it. Robin couldn't have cared less.'

Mary decided to ignore this, musing reminiscently, 'I remember the day when old man Ryland was more than content with two small mills.'

Celia broke in bitterly, 'Until his son grew up and decided they should establish themselves in the retail trade, cutting out the middle man and selling their own goods.'

'You must admit it's paid off. Guy Ryland will be no pauper, I'm willing to bet!'

'And no one would take you on! Of course we all know he's well off, but what sort of man could enjoy his wealth

17

knowing the accumulating of it had meant the ruination of those who had previously brought from him? Guy Ryland, and men like him, could come to rue the day ...'

An audible sigh escaped Mary at the sight of Celia's flushed, resentful face. Attempting to pour oil on troubled waters, she tried to be tactful. 'It's usually unavoidable that someone suffers, but I still believe Guy acted in the only possible way. There are many I can think of who wouldn't have shown the same consideration.'

'So you said.' Celia's face remained mutinous.

'Perhaps it's a pity you ever left Manchester,' Mary surprised her by saying reflectively.

'You're a fine one to talk,' Celia grinned, feeling a sudden need to have the conversation lighter, 'seeing how you never cared for the place yourself.'

'But I'm not you, darling,' Mary pointed out with seeming logic. 'I was never exactly a native of the place. Your mother and I just visited your grandparents. I was born here in London.'

'You're probably just tired of having me around, then,' Celia persisted, oddly perverse.

'You know I'm not,' Mary spoke anxiously. 'I certainly didn't mean to give that impression.'

Momentarily Celia felt ashamed of herself. She had known exactly what Mary was talking about, she had no reason to pretend not to understand. 'I'm sorry,' she apologised contritely, 'I guess I can be a bit of a pig when I feel like it.'

Mary laughed, completely forgiving. Who couldn't forgive Celia anything when she looked at you like that! 'But you will go home for Christmas?' she asked, more anxiously than she knew.

'I don't know.'

'Is it your work?'

'Not really. There's nothing I can't leave. Nothing, I suppose, to keep me at the moment.'

If Mary was surprised she managed successfully to hide

it. Celia had always considered herself dedicated to her work. Now her manner suggested it was of no real importance. 'Well, then?' she prompted, hating to sound persistent, but some haunting, forlorn look, barely discernible in the depth of the girl's eyes, seemed to urge her on.

She knew she was right when Celia sighed. It was only a faint sound, trembling softly on unsteady young lips, and if Mary hadn't been all attention she might not have heard it. It hinted of a bewilderment of spirit, an uncertain confusion, unconsciously confirming Mary's suspicions that she was far from happy. What strange mixture of emotions had driven her from her home three years ago, the older woman wondered, not for the first time. Careerwise Celia might have achieved success, but clearly otherwise she had gained very little.

'I think,' Celia said slowly, as if forcing herself to a reluctant decision, 'I ought to go for a few days, anyway. For Lucy's sake. I don't see how I can refuse.'

'Not only for Lucy,' agreed Mary.

Celia's smile hid an almost visible uneasiness. 'For my own sake, too,' she confessed. 'It's maybe high time I laid a few ghosts, although I'm not sure where I should start. All my instincts point in the direction of Manchester, but I could be so wrong. I'm probably just suffering from a mild dose of homesickness. Who can tell?'

Such frankness, while partly enigmatical, did seem a step in the right direction. Swiftly encouraging, Mary replied, 'Lucy and Robin will be delighted.'

'And so will you—even more so.' This time the curve of Celia's lips deepened to a real smile. Mary could be endearingly transparent. 'Will you come with me, darling?' she rushed on before Mary could speak. 'Robin especially asked.'

'No ...' Mary had her excuses all ready. 'I think I'm going down to Torquay. Jenny Linton has asked me twice. I was actually just about to mention it when Robin rang. I should love to see her.'

19

'I see. Well then——' Doubtful still, Celia glanced at her aunt quickly. She hated to think that for some reason Mary didn't feel welcome, but obviously Manchester had no appeal, and she had known and worked with Jenny Linton for years. 'If you're quite sure,' she went on ruefully, 'I might go a day or two earlier and give Timmy a hand. Lucy is at the shop and Robin expects she'll be busy right up until Christmas Eve.'

Relieved that Celia had finally made up her mind, Mary said happily, 'Mrs Timpson is so efficient. I'm sure you'll find there's not much to do.'

'No, of course not,' Celia laughed, feeling her heart suddenly lighter in spite of her apprehension about Lucy and her own affairs. 'But I love to help, you know that, and at Christmas there's always so much to be done. I know, for instance, that poor old Timmy doesn't care for holly and decorations. The putting of them up, I mean.'

Thinking about it she couldn't restrain a note of eager anticipation. Christmas at Number Nine Moorland Road, the large but far from smart old terrace house in what once had been a fashionable area of Manchester. It was something she had never thought to look forward to again. Not once since her father died had she felt like this. It was as if the difficult momentum of her decision had removed some of the painful ache from around her heart, allowing a glimpse of the young, almost carefree girl she could scarcely remember.

There was so much, yet so little to keep her in London. So far as her work went she hadn't been entirely unsuccessful. When she had first arrived she had carried a letter for the manager of a large West End firm, a personal friend of her father's. He had given her a job, but by her own ability she had established herself as one of their best models. It was something she had never attempted previously—an exclusive job with an exclusive establishment which left her a certain amount of scope for freelance work. Nothing spectacular, but what she had done had proved sufficiently satisfactory. She had just finished a toothpaste job for TV commercials and another for soap because, so she had been told, she had a fabulous skin.

Mary intruded on the wavering fragments of thought. 'After Christmas,' she said, 'you'll be going straight off to Bermuda, so I might stay in Torquay until you return.'

Celia hid a swift smile of amusement. That Mary didn't altogether approve of the swimsuit job in such an exotic part of the world had been obvious from the start, although she hadn't said so outright. The fact that it was for one of the top fashion magazines had carried no influence whatsoever. Celia herself, though she would be reluctant to admit it, wasn't all that keen to go.

It had been something inside her, some small, desperate voice urging her on, which had forced a final commitment. One of the photographers whom she was beginning to know rather well had almost begged her to accept. Joe, she was well aware, was half in love with her, would like an affair with her, but she always said no—why, she wasn't at all certain. Perhaps because she hated being too personally involved with a man. Ever since Guy Ryland had touched her there had been a feeling of distaste. Sometimes she felt as if the shock of his hands were still with her, their grip on her wrists keeping her transfixed in a half-frozen state by remote control. All of which would have sounded too far-fetched to explain to anyone, even if she could have found words sufficiently suitable to express such fanciful notions.

'You can't remain as you are for ever, sweetheart,' Joe had said more than once, well aware of her untouched aura if not the root cause of it.

She never minded Joe's remarks because she liked him, and had decided that at twenty-three it was perhaps time she began to think seriously about a man. A lack of experience could prove a certain handicap to a girl in some circles. Some sort of decision was definitely called for, but it could be safely shelved until after Christmas. By then she might have laid her particular ghost and Bermuda might be something she could really look forward to!

She came back with a new, comforting certainty to Aunt Mary who was repeating again very patiently that she would stay in Torquay. 'You do that, darling,' she smiled. 'I can always give you a ring when I return from Bermuda.'

It was snowing in Manchester, great flakes of thick, fluffy snow falling softly, muting the sound of heavy traffic, doing much to hide beneath a carpeting whiteness the grey, uncompromising precincts of the city. It wouldn't stay long; tomorrow there could be only drear slush, odd pools of half-frozen muddy water, but while it lasted a snowstorm did add enormously to the festive spirit.

Celia hadn't said which day she was coming, as she hadn't been exactly sure when she could get away. Lucy, when she rang, had said not to worry. Her bed was ready—just so long as she didn't change her mind. This was the important thing. There had seemed a hint of pathos in Lucy's voice which would have made such an event impossible. Caught off guard, Celia had been forced to swallow a sudden lump in her throat before promising faithfully that she would be there.

Now, standing gazing at the dark old house where they had all been born, Celia found herself almost regretting such promises. She had managed to stay away nearly three years, and if she hadn't been so easily diverted she wouldn't have been standing here in the gathering, snow-filled dusk realising how much she had missed every inch of it. Tears, glittering with the tiny particles of snow on her long lashes, emphasised the sapphire blueness of her eyes. Those weeks prior to her leaving had been too full of pain and apprehension to have left any room for nostalgia. And since then, she had clung to the conclusion that she hated the north. Until this moment!

Tense with a peculiar bewilderment, Celia covered the narrow front drive which could scarcely be called a drive

22

proper, as the house was set only about ten yards back from the road. The taxi which had brought her from the station drove away, leaving her quite alone. She was safe no longer. Feeling completely vulnerable and seized by a great agitation, she turned her face once more towards the narrow, deep-set windows from which the dim yellow light of a dubious welcome shone out. She squared her slim shoulders, and from the depths of her handbag she took her key and inserted it in the lock. Taking a deep breath, she nervously opened the door and let herself in, closing it swiftly behind her again.

CHAPTER TWO

THE hall was deserted and darker than Celia remembered, steeped in shadow, the centre light dim. From the study came the sound of low voices. She had noticed Robin's car standing in the drive as she came in. Probably he was there with Lucy, having tea.

Swiftly, feeling the need of some herself, she crossed over the square of red carpet. She noted that it was becoming threadbare, but the thought barely registered, so keen was she to see them both again. She didn't knock—surely it was unnecessary even if she had been away a long time. She was their sister, not some casual acquaintance who had just dropped in.

Quietly, almost holding her breath with a sudden warm excitement, she turned the old-fashioned doorknob, pausing expectantly in the doorway. It was a moment laced with freezing drama. As her head came up she found herself gazing straight into the eyes of Guy Ryland.

For long seconds she seemed unable to move, to do anything else but stare at him as the first shock waves moved through her. The days, the years, the years between their first and last meeting might never have existed, and the thought was like a blow, threatening her fragile peace. All the time she had accumulated as a certain insurance against him was proved useless. Yet it might just be a case of mind over matter. Pride and convention demanded that she found her voice.

'I beg your pardon. I seem to be intruding.'

It was Robin who broke the unbearable tension. 'Why, Celia!' he exclaimed, his thin face lighting up as he turned and saw her. 'Of course not. Come in!'

It took an almost exhausting effort to pull herself together, to clamp down on a too vivid imagination and move into the room. It was a dreadful thing to be too aware of a man standing watching; too aware that the mental picture she had carried for so long seemed in every minute detail correct. The dark, enigmatical face—the tall, lean, powerfully built body. The whole impression was one of force, of controlled vitality. His mouth, she saw, was twisted with a faint satisfaction, as though he likened her fluttering state to the strivings of a moth against a light, guaranteed to return to its final destruction. His cool, level gaze held an element of triumph.

'I'm sorry.' Desperately she wrenched her eyes away, attempting to concentrate on Robin, but in spite of her endeavour her words came stiffly. 'I should have let you know I was arriving—the exact time, I mean. I can see you're busy.'

'It doesn't matter,' Robin assured her again, 'we were expecting you.' Then, as his glance swung back to the man by his side, he continued in a rush, almost as if he shared some of his sister's embarrassment, 'I don't think you've met Guy.'

'Not officially.' For the first time Guy Ryland spoke, although his eyes had never once left Celia's face since she walked through the doorway. Now, as he smoothly supplied the answer to Robin's question, his appraising glance rested

24

speculatively on the long, slim legs, the small perfect head on the stem-like neck, the swing of tawny, shining hair about slender shoulders. Celia had the sudden crazy notion that he regarded her like one of the eastern slave-owners of old speculating over a purchase, something which already belonged to him by some simple ancient law of declaration.

Robin, apparently confused by something slightly incomprehensible in his employer's manner, was heard to repeat curiously, 'Not officially?'

Guy obviously had no intention of explaining fully. He said lightly, 'I only caught a glimpse of your sister for a few minutes. We were never properly introduced.'

'Celia,' Robin frowned, 'hasn't been home for ages.'

'No, I'm quite aware of it. It was a long time ago, but I assure you she wasn't as tongue-tied as she appears to be now.'

Decisively he placed the half-empty glass he held on the mantelpiece, and crossed the floor to where she stood, his hand extended. A gesture of cordiality, an outward pretence of friendship entirely for Robin's benefit, Celia fancied wildly.

But because she remembered Robin's inborn curiosity and instinctively, as of old, sought to avoid it, she took the proffered hand—very coolly, as if she hoped to transmit a lack of warmth, a definite message through the indifferent touch of her fingers. 'I scarcely remember Mr Ryland at all,' she said recklessly and, had she but known it, quite foolishly.

The mockery in Guy Ryland's eyes following that misleading little speech was barely to be tolerated.

Robin, as usual doing things the wrong way around, was stumbling belatedly over names, performing the necessary introductions, and nervousness aroused in Celia a fine irritation. 'We hope she'll stay for Christmas,' he was saying, seemingly to the floor. 'I don't know why she ever went away.'

'Who knows?' Guy Ryland replied suavely, 'But we

might indeed profit from her experience.'

Which might have sounded ponderous coming from any-one else, but Celia read the double meaning in his remark that naturally escaped Robin. There was the additional, un-spoken implication that the three years Guy referred to so glibly had been allowed magnanimously. A period for her to grow into the kind of woman he liked having around. She felt it involuntarily that he had never com-pletely lost sight of her, but far from feeling flattered she was suddenly filled with apprehension, an underlying terror. Her eyes travelled again down the length of him before returning to meet his, and almost visibly, before she could stop herself, she shuddered. Swiftly her dark lashes fell, refusing to sustain his calculating glance indefinitely.

'I will most certainly be staying until after Christmas,' she forced herself to say deliberately, 'but I have work to do in Bermuda, so I'll probably be leaving immediately after-wards.'

At this, Guy Ryland laughed. 'I think,' he spoke to Robin directly, 'between us we might persuade her to change her mind.'

Celia's pulse throbbed out some sort of warning. She knew a clear and vivid, if totally incomprehensible, sensa-tion of panic. On the face of it Guy had just passed a re-mark of ordinary politeness, but his tone suggested it went deeper than that. She was struck by the conviction that he was putting into motion some long-anticipated plan. His words contained, for Robin's benefit, a subtle threat that his collaboration should be given—or else! A new and frightening dimension seemed to be emerging. Guy Ryland would reward those who served him well, just so long as they were willing to dance to his tune!

He was standing very still, his eyes, brilliant and mock-ing, fixed narrowly on her. He reminded her of some sleek animal, basking in her uncertainty, knowing some form of amusement was well within reach. Uneasily she stared away from him. Maybe she was letting an overheated imagination play tricks on her, but before anyone got any wrong ideas perhaps she ought to make the purpose of her visit doubly clear.

Firmly she said, 'I came specially to see Lucy. You, too,' she added, smiling swiftly at Robin in case he felt hurt. 'But I do have a job to return to, so my visit must necessarily be brief.'

Robin, for some reason, was beginning to look far from comfortable, glancing nervously at Guy, which exasperated Celia completely.

'Where is Lucy?' she inquired swiftly, saving him the trouble of a suitable comment. She was suddenly curious as to Guy Ryland's reactions when she mentioned Lucy, and as she didn't intend to see him again, she might never get another opportunity. Robin could have missed a lot of clues which would immediately be obvious to a woman.

Robin let out a swift breath, as if relieved to be once more on familiar ground. 'She doesn't finish until after five, you know. Guy ran me home early as there was something he wanted to discuss.'

So it wasn't Robin's car in the drive. Celia wondered suddenly if he had one. Guy Ryland didn't add to his short statement, and a quick glance at his dark face revealed nothing. Perhaps Robin had been right after all? Guy's indifferent expression hadn't changed one little bit at the mention of Lucy's name. He must not suspect anything.

'She probably won't be long,' Robin was murmuring, misunderstanding her flickering frown.

'Oh, I'm not worrying,' she returned lightly, 'I know how it is. And as you and Mr Ryland have business matters to talk over, I'll go and say hello to Timmy. I expect I'll find her in the kitchen.'

It was annoying that her reasonable attitude should make Robin choke slightly, his expression announcing this was all getting too much for him. Nor did he look any happier when Guy Ryland suggested softly, 'I would advise you to talk over your domestic affairs after I've gone,

Robin. But before I leave you might like to tell Celia about my invitation.'

His invitation? Momentarily diverted, Celia's eyes widened with some alarm. Surely he didn't have the audacity to include her in any of his activities!

Robin visibly brightened. 'Guy has asked us all to spend Christmas with him,' he smiled. 'I realise you've only just arrived, but I'm sure you'll be happy to accept. There's nothing to keep you here.'

For one blank moment surprise held Celia silent. Bleak anger flickered in her shadowed eyes. Trust Robin to take so much for granted! She had envisaged a cosy Christmas; just the three of them with Timmy. This was like a slap in the face. In her cheeks bright colour flared, then faded, leaving her quite pale. Where was Robin's pride? She herself might have too much, but rather that than too little! Not content to be taken over by this man Ryland, to devoting what must be some of the best years of his life to him, Robin now allowed him to dictate how he spent his leisure time!

'I'm sure you would enjoy a brief break at my country house.' Guy, apparently turning a blind eye to Celia's indignant face, added smoothly to his invitation before she could recover sufficiently to announce exactly what she thought of it. 'Robin and Lucy are delighted.'

'But I shouldn't be! I shouldn't even think of going!' she breathed as he paused. 'I came back to spend Christmas in my home, not yours.' She finished coldly, her blue eyes, sparkling with dislike, meeting his with determination. There was also a strange hurt that Robin and Lucy had done this to her.

'I'm sorry, Celia ...' Robin, not usually sensitive, was suddenly aware of her feelings. 'I really did think you would be pleased. At least,' he amended lamely, 'I didn't think you would mind.' Apologetically he glanced towards Guy Ryland.

Celia treated this to the contempt she considered it de-

28

served. Robin, she was quick to realise, was a mere pawn in the game. Not that she knew yet what Guy Ryland's game was—not exactly! But Robin, she guessed instinctively, was in Guy Ryland's estimation of no consequence other than on the odd occasion when he could be useful. Deliberately she ignored him, keeping her eyes on Robin.

'Naturally,' she said swiftly, 'I shan't interfere with any plans you've already made, but I can assure you—and Mr Ryland—that I shall stay here with Mrs Timpson.'

Again there was silence, although the quality of it in each man varied. Robin's was still plainly uncomfortable, while Guy Ryland's contained the sardonic complacency of one who is satisfied that the victim is almost within his reach.

'There's nothing wrong in staying with Mrs Timpson, is there?' she challenged mistakenly, when neither man spoke.

Coldly she tilted her chin, and it seemed Guy Ryland remembered that defiant gesture. His dark face swam above her, lightly ironical. His eyes moved over her, pleasantly satirical, as if he enjoyed being cruel. 'I think you'd better get your sister a drink, Robin,' he said softly. 'You're going to need it,' he assured her as she started to protest. 'Your Mrs Timmy, as you call her, now works for me.'

Celia could never recollect being so shocked, so incredulous. Not dear old Timmy, she could never believe it of her! 'You can't be serious?' she spluttered, pushing aside the drink Robin tried to place in her shaking hands. 'Why, she's always been here!'

'Not any more, I'm afraid.' Guy Ryland was between them, muttering something in Robin's ear, and Robin disappeared.

'Where has he gone?' she cried, her eyes smouldering blue fire, fuelled by the terrible feeling of being trapped.

'Simply to make some tea,' Guy Ryland replied, his impudence making her physically breathless. 'Don't worry, he'll be back in a minute, and I shall leave you to have a

29

nice cosy chat. Lucy ought to be here by then.'

She attacked him wildly. 'So now we have to look after ourselves! How dared you steal Timmy?'

He at once became coolly detached, not willing to be cross-questioned in this fashion, and his firm mouth thinned. 'She was looking for a job,' he allowed briefly. 'I gave her one. It was as simple as that.'

Celia couldn't entertain this, not for a minute. Timmy was a wonderful housekeeper, a perfect cook. It hadn't taken him long to realise she was an asset to be acquired, just like the shop! This man's methods were devious, he must have enticed her away with something Timmy had been unable to resist, even though it had meant leaving Robin and Lucy without help.

Such was the force of her despair that discretion deserted her. 'So as well as a thief you're a liar,' she cried. 'I know Timmy wouldn't leave of her own accord.'

Something like anger touched his hard face, of a sudden he was remote, a stranger. But only for a second. Then his expression changed to the semblance of cool humour, although she was sure no hint of a smile ever reached his eyes. 'You still haven't forgotten, have you, Miss Kingsley?'

No, her heart cried, I haven't forgotten. You only had to touch my hand to bring it all back—this thing I seem unable to escape from. But it could only, she assured herself, be hate! She said, sullenly, not pretending to misinterpret him, 'Some things one doesn't easily forget, and I didn't expect to find you here this evening.'

'Obviously not,' he agreed briefly. 'We seem to have got off on the wrong footing.'

'Something your PRO wouldn't approve of,' she flashed.

'My public relations men are used to dealing with reasonable people,' he replied calmly, laying the fault adroitly on her own doorstep. 'I would have thought three years long enough for any girl to grow up.'

'My state of mind, adolescent or otherwise, can be of no interest to you, Mr Ryland.' Refusing to be browbeaten,

30

she kept her young voice deliberately impertinent. Much better that he should assume she was naturally slightly insolent. It might at least provide some sort of barrier against his overriding masculinity. 'The mere fact,' she rushed on, 'that I object to your methods apparently condemns me in your eyes.'

He sighed roughly, still staring at her, his mouth hardening again as he watched her. He found her insistence tedious and made little attempt to disguise the fact. 'If you insist on mulling over the past, you force me to tell you that Robin was no longer in a position to afford someone like Mrs Timpson.'

Celia was far from convinced. 'Money was never important to Timmy,' she declared.

'I refuse to argue.' Suddenly adamant, he straightened as if already he regretted offering any kind of explanation. 'I daresay your brother will be better able than I to fill in the domestic details.'

Such things would be beneath him, Celia inwardly sneered, holding a fine contempt firmly over another more complex emotion. 'I'm sure he will,' she rejoined tartly. 'Don't let me keep you, Mr Ryland, unless, of course, you still want to see my brother about something?'

'It will keep.' He was back again to a cool civility as he walked to the door. There he turned, pausing significantly. 'I shall expect you with the others on Christmas Eve, Miss Kingsley. Make sure you turn up.'

'I suppose he's gone?' Robin said warily a few minutes later when he arrived with a tray of tea.

'Thanks be for that at least!' Robin's arrival seemed to release Celia from a state of frozen incredulity, but she was unable to keep the bitterness from her voice. Jumping up, she began quickly to arrange the cups and saucers which he had piled haphazardly, but found it almost impossible to look at the tea because it had been Guy Ryland's idea. 'Shouldn't we wait for Lucy?' she asked, ignoring Robin's

31

uncomfortable expression. His face was too like a barometer for his own good!

'Lucy,' he grimaced, collapsing exhausted into the nearest chair, 'won't be home for quite a while.'

'But why not?' Celia stared at him, frowning.

Robin seemed to give up, as if the effort of coping with two sisters was suddenly too much for him. He said frankly, 'She's out with the boy-friend, only I daren't tell Guy.'

'You mean Denis Ryland?'

'Precisely,' Robin shrugged. 'And before you start to read the riot act, I might remind you there are limits to any brother's authority. She is after all a free agent, and over twenty-one.'

'You don't have to sound so prosaic,' Celia said tersely. 'I know I'm in no position to criticise, but I can't really admire the way you seem to have handled things. You probably couldn't stop her, but didn't you point out how foolish she was being, encouraging a Ryland?'

Robin threw back his fair head and raised his blue eyes, so like Celia's, to the ceiling. A man praying for patience!

'Of course I did,' he assured her, 'but you don't imagine for one minute that it's made any difference?'

'But surely she must realise how despicable these Rylands can be? I don't seem to remember a Denis Ryland, but I don't doubt he's just as bad as the rest of them.'

'Not everyone,' Robin pointed out mildly, 'would share your views. Besides, Denis hasn't been with the firm for more than a few months. He isn't even much of a cousin, I believe. I've heard that his name is almost the only evidence of relationship, he's so far removed, but as there aren't any others around I suppose Guy couldn't be too choosy.'

She had no idea what Robin implied by that, nor did she care. 'I should have thought even a slight connection makes him something to be avoided.'

Robin's mouth twisted as his hand went up wryly to loosen his tie. 'Confidentially, I believe Lucy thinks so, too.

32

As a matter of fact—if you can't wait to hear it from her, I mean the full story—they'd met a few times before she realised exactly who he was, and by then, so I'm told, it was too late.'

'Too late—for what?'

'Celia darling, are you intentionally dense?' Robin's face was a study of weary exasperation and he gazed with some longing at the teapot, still standing exactly where he had put it down. 'They happen to be in love, if you know what that means, and Lucy is actually no keener than you about it, although for different reasons.'

'Different reasons?' Celia's brain whirled, trying to keep pace. Some of Robin's enigmatic statements were far from clear.

'Well, to begin with, she's not at all sure that Denis's affections are strong enough to withstand Guy's persuasions.'

'In what way?'

'All I'm prepared to say is that there's another girl, whose father is comparatively wealthy. She, it seems, has taken quite a fancy to Denis Ryland, and it's no secret that Guy favours such a union.'

'Surely with all his money it couldn't really matter!' Celia's voice rang with undisguised scorn. 'And if Guy is so keen to add to the Ryland fortunes, why can't he marry the girl himself?'

'A good question.' As if finding a grain of humour in the situation, Robin suddenly grinned. 'One which plenty of other people have asked besides yourself. Guy was around thirty-four when Father died, which should make him now about thirty-seven, and it might be argued that he has more than most to offer.'

'Then why doesn't he, do you think?' Celia heard herself persisting, while trying to ignore a twinge of unaccountable pain.

'Why should he?' Robin laughed, with all the complacency of a confirmed bachelor. 'He enjoys a good time. Why

33

sacrifice his freedom if he can use someone else to attain what he wants? The frightening thing is,' he sobered completely, 'he usually gets what he wants in the end.'

Swiftly apprehensive, Celia's glance flew to her brother's face. She could recall Guy Ryland quite clearly; the lines etched about his mouth and eyes, did they speak of a dedication to work, or pleasure? Maybe, she thought, quickly disparaging, a mixture of both. There would be enough of him to stand the strain. Before she could stop herself she shuddered, and alarmed by the disquieting intensity of her feelings she tried to concentrate on something else.

It was as her eyes turned rather helplessly back to Robin's amateurish efforts with the tea-tray that she remembered Mrs Timpson. 'You haven't told me yet,' she said, 'about Mrs Timpson. Exactly why did she have to go?'

'To be perfectly frank,' Robin replied, as Celia passed him a half-cold cup of tea, 'I just couldn't afford to keep her.'

'Not keep her! But you must be earning a decent salary?'

'I am,' Robin was not blind to the sudden frown on Celia's face, 'but you know how it is! What with tax and one thing and another. There's the rent, you see, and rates, before I even begin . . .'

'Rent?' Celia's voice faded to a mere whisper. 'But you own the house, surely?'

'What makes you think so?'

'Well, Daddy told me . . .'

'Everything but this, I expect,' Robin said wryly. 'It was his for his lifetime, then it went back to Ryland's.'

'But you never said!' Celia's face was strangely white, her hands shaking slightly.

'Did you ever give me a chance! You were in such an all-fired hurry to get back to London.'

Put like that, it made her sound the most selfish person on earth! Perhaps she was? Dazed, Celia stared at him uncomprehending. One shock was following another and none of them she liked. She had flown back to London fully aware that there was nothing left, but not wanting to know how little. Childishly she had fled that first time, cowardice had driven her the next. No other word could describe her headlong flight.

She saw quite clearly now that she ought to have stayed and shared some of the problems which must have almost devastated a man like Robin. The full burden of being left to deal single-handed with the legacy of a ruined estate and the capricious moods of a bewildered young Lucy.

'I'm sorry, Robin,' she managed at last, and sensing the total inadequacy of those two words, adding futilely, 'I didn't realise.'

Robin made no immediate reply apart from his customary shrug. Obviously not much given to harbouring grudges, he didn't seem bitter. Some sixth sense warned Celia that he was more anxious about the future.

Biting her full bottom lip hard, she succeeded in keeping back further explanations which might only have sounded like more excuses. She also refrained, with some difficulty, from asking more questions about Mrs Timpson. She could always tackle Lucy about her later. Instead she asked, her voice surprisingly humble, 'You do still have your job at the shop?'

'At this moment,' Robin grunted morosely, 'and I hope to keep it.'

'Is there any reason,' Celia floundered, 'why you shouldn't?'

'Plenty,' he replied, his usually cheerful face sober, 'if Lucy does the wrong thing and you don't do the right one.'

Celia stared at him. 'Robin,' she began, anxiously impatient, 'that doesn't make sense.'

'I mean—if Lucy continues with her mad romance, and you continue to refuse Guy's Christmas invitation, between the two of you I could be sunk. It maybe doesn't make sense to you, but I can see the writing plainly on the wall.'

'You must be joking!' she exclaimed in stark disbelief, 'About both of us. Lucy is surely old enough to realise exactly what she's doing, and I'm certainly under no obligation to fall in with any of Guy Ryland's plans! Why don't you find another job, Robin? I'm sure you could find plenty without having to rely on a man like that.'

Robin's face grew stubborn. Celia remembered the look. 'I'd never find another position like it,' he declared. 'I'm practically boss of the whole show. Guy spends very little time there.'

'You mean you're still a sort of managing director?' Celia's brows creased with far from flattering surprise.

'Well—not exactly, but just as long as things are running smoothly Guy seldom interferes. We don't see very much of him. He has plenty of other things to keep him busy without bothering me.'

The slight touch of self-importance didn't escape her. Unless it was simply self-confidence, which could help him in other ways. 'If you can do a job like this, Robin, then you could probably find a similar position anywhere,' she suggested.

A sarcastic grin quirked on his lips. 'You can't be serious!' he jeered. 'With the present rate of unemployment, what chance would I stand? I don't even possess any proper qualifications, and I'm over thirty.'

'But to be so completely dependent on Guy Ryland!'

'So what!' Robin's patience was fraying a bit around the edges. 'It suits me very well, I can assure you. I would never find anything as convenient so near.'

Celia stared at him, fighting back the recurring bitterness she found so hard to conceal. Where had all this enthusiasm been three years ago? Even a little of it might have saved something of the business their grandfather and father had worked so hard to build.

'About this Christmas party,' Robin went on, as if determined to make his position clear. 'Couldn't you just swallow your pride, if that's what's stopping you, and go? If you don't . . .' his voice trailed off dismally.

'Yes?' she prompted sharply. 'If I don't?'

Robin glanced at her unhappily, as if he really understood the situation no more than she did. 'If you don't,' he repeated, parrot-wise, 'then I'm very much afraid I shall be looking for this new job you talk of in the New Year!'

It was almost midnight before she went to bed, but it was not until the early hours that she heard Lucy come in. From the downstairs rooms Celia had removed any evidence of her arrival, and as she heard the girl creeping quietly along the corridor outside her bedroom door, she was aware that Lucy wouldn't know she was there.

Celia didn't call her. Robin had talked so long, and so disconcertingly, that she felt she couldn't bear any more right then. There would be heaps of time in the morning or later in the day when Lucy returned from work. If she stopped Lucy now there would probably only be something else to trouble her already guilt-laden conscience. At the moment it was so over-burdened that Celia was unable to sleep.

Robin had been enough! Once started he had talked so much, and made it abundantly clear that she had been needed here more than she had ever dreamt. If only she could have closed her ears to him! Yet it hadn't actually been what he said, but rather the bits he had missed out. How could she continue to reproach him about either the shop or Lucy, when perhaps her own selfishness might be proved worse than his!

At about seven she had made a light meal. Robin said there was a pie in the fridge. She found the remains of one, and the rather scrappy meal she managed to prepare had filled her with dismay. Lucy might somehow manage to exist on such meagre rations, but there was nothing here to satisfy a man.

She hadn't been in any way reassured when Robin declared that he didn't mind. 'I don't eat a lot,' he had shrugged, 'and I do have a good lunch at the shop, so I don't starve.'

Which didn't seem to Celia a very satisfactory way to

37

live at all, even if Robin appeared to find nothing wrong with it. She must see that the larder and store cupboard was filled for Christmas. At least it would keep her busy, give her something to do. The idea that she mightn't be spending Christmas here, now that she was home, was not to be tolerated!

When she did eventually sleep, Celia slept heavily until after eight and woke with a start to find Lucy bending over her.

'Wake up, darling,' she cried, giving Celia a slight shake. 'Would you believe it, Robin has just told me you're here. I might have left for work without knowing!'

With an effort Celia raised a sleep-drenched smile. Lucy's radiance, after what could only have been an hour or two in bed, startled her. Did love do this for a girl? 'Your own fault,' she mumbled, as Lucy lightly kissed her cheek. Then—'Don't let me detain you. Maybe, like Robin, you live in fear of instant dismissal?'

'Oh, dear,' Lucy giggled, 'if you'd been up I might have said you'd tumbled from the wrong side of your bed. Anyone who looks like you at this time of the morning has no right to be cross at all.'

'I'm just not,' Celia tried again, 'in the mood . . .'

'Never mind. It's lovely to see you. I'm sorry I was out.'

'So was I.'

'I'll see you tonight,' Lucy exclaimed, with a swift glance of mock dismay at her watch. 'I don't live in fear of instant dismissal, as you so terrifyingly put it, but right at this moment I'm not taking any risks. I shan't be late.'

She was gone before Celia could find her next breath, and scrambling quickly to the window she was just in time to see Lucy departing with Robin below. So Robin did have a car, and quite a smart one at that, by the looks of it. She had intended to ask, but they had been so busy talking. Lucy, as if aware of being watched, looked up, and nudged Robin who also glanced up, and they both waved. Celia waved back as they drove through the gate.

Frowning as she watched them go, she remained standing by the window. Did some demon in the form of Guy Ryland drive them on? Was he behind this astonishing desire to get to work on time, or was it merely a somewhat belated attack of adult responsibility? A whole lot, she realised, could happen in three years. Things might change, but so did people. Robin and Lucy were not exactly as she remembered them; Lucy had grown up, and Robin seemed too full of a nervous apprehension about his job at the shop. Celia felt a quick shudder run through her lightly clad body as she wondered what other disturbing elements her few days' holiday might reveal.

Now that they had left she found she couldn't go back to bed, so she swiftly washed and dressed and ran downstairs. There was a great desire within her to be busy, she didn't want any time to think. In the kitchen the kettle was still warm, and she merely switched it on again to boil it up. With a huge mug of tea clasped in her hand she decided to go through the house.

It was still barely daylight, the rather grim winter's morning heavily overcast. Outside, as she had guessed, the snow had already started to thaw, and a cold greyness shrouded the neighbouring houses, wrapping everything in icy gloom. Not a very inviting prospect, but then Manchester at this time of year rarely was, and Celia refused to let the bleak outlook depress her.

Even in two years the house seemed to have shrunk surprisingly. Possibly due to its new owner, she thought, prepared to be unreasonable. So far as Guy Ryland was concerned she felt unable to be anything else, but it was still difficult to believe that a firm like Ryland's would even bother to consider such an old-fashioned house. She must see the family lawyer herself. She would make an immediate appointment. Robin was so very gullible. Up against the characteristically cunning Rylands he wouldn't stand a chance. Failing this, she would have it out with Guy

39

Ryland himself. No one was going to steal her family home unless it was absolutely legal!

Her mind only half on what she was doing, Celia toured the low, dark rooms, occupied by thoughts which she might in other circumstances have considered peculiar, but as these particular ones were centred on Guy Ryland she didn't think of them in this context at all. The house, it barely registered, was reasonably clean but very untidy. Lucy's bedroom appeared never to have been sorted out for weeks and Robin's wasn't much better. Everything, she noticed, was getting shabbier. Daddy, she recalled, had always been going to redecorate, refurbish, but somehow it had never been done, always it had managed to last another year.

Celia missed Timmy. Timmy had always possessed the happy knack of being able to cheer one up. Back in the kitchen, her tour of inspection over, she gazed moodily at the one-bar electric fire which seemed to be the standard form of heating throughout the entire house. No longer did large log fires burn in the wide fireplaces. These appeared to have been boarded up and out of use for a long time, as when she had tried to remove the board from the sitting-room fireplace she had discovered the back chock-full of dust and cobwebs.

Wistfully she thought of Mrs Timpson. She wouldn't have tolerated such contraptions. She would have had a fire going in no time, and the house looking so cheerful and lived-in that no one would have noticed the shabbiness of the surroundings. Somehow Celia couldn't imagine Christmas without her. And yet—making a stupendous effort, Celia tried to shake off her self-pity. How many households could afford help of any kind these days, let alone someone living in? Mr Ryland was indeed fortunate!

Despite herself, Celia was truly depressed, and tried for the remainder of the morning to restore what Aunt Mary was fond of calling a lived-in look to the place. The daily woman didn't arrive and there was no other help, and having no natural aptitude for work of this nature Celia soon realised she was fighting a losing battle. Gazing with some bewilderment at her slender white fingers immersed in the third kettleful of hot soda water, she decided she had been spoiled. During the last three years in London she had done very little domestic work, thanks, chiefly, to Mary's efficiency when it came to such matters. If she had been here she would have known exactly how to go about things, and what to do.

Celia's brows crinkled as she raised her blue eyes from her wet hands and stared around the hall where she was kneeling. She had been working steadily for over two hours and there seemed no vast improvement. It all looked much as it had done when she had started!

Suddenly, very miserably, she began to regret that she had ever come back, or that she had ever gone away in the first place. Either way she could have avoided this kind of heartache. And so desperate were her thoughts that when the telephone rang from the hall table almost on top of her, she grasped it like a positive lifeline, taking no notice of the tears which perversely streamed down her face and dripped on to the receiver.

CHAPTER THREE

CELIA's fingers tightened around the receiver. 'Celia Kingsley here,' she said, her voice blurred in the manner of one who is crying. She only expected Robin or Lucy, or perhaps Aunt Mary, who would be wondering if she had arrived safely, and whom Celia had intended to ring. Submerged in the confusing difficulties of her homecoming she had forgotten. Now, ruefully ashamed of herself, she prepared to apologise, but it was none of these people. It was Guy Ryland.

41

'Are you busy?' he inquired, his question giving an impression of intimacy which annoyed.

'Yes,' she answered abruptly, wondering why on earth he should ring.

There was a fraction of silence. 'You sound upset.' His voice sharpened. 'Is there anything wrong?'

Drawing a deeply steadying breath, she controlled her tears with difficulty, not willing to confirm his obvious suspicions or to allow him to think she was looking for a shoulder to cry on. 'No,' she said.

He made no further comment. Instead he asked, copying her own abruptness, 'Will you have lunch with me?'

'Lunch with you? No!' Her surprised exclamation was in direct conflict with another part of her which derisively pointed out the empty larder. 'I'm sorry,' she snapped, managing to ignore her completely shameless pangs of hunger.

'You could be,' his tone was caustic, as if he guessed the depleted state of her store cupboard, 'but in this instance I'm going to leave you with little choice. There are things we must discuss. I shall pick you up in about an hour.'

'Why——' It was all she got out before the line went dead. Until it hurt, and she fully realised what she was doing, Celia sat biting her lip. It was all a bit beyond her, this presumptuous summons which she somehow felt unable to ignore. It couldn't concern her personally so must be about Robin or Lucy, which left her, as he said, little choice. He had been crafty enough to time his call well, astute enough to know that after several hours alone in a cold, empty house, she would be almost ready to agree to anything. Contrary to all her half-formed hopes and expectations there was no real sense of being home.

Swiftly, surrendering reluctantly to circumstances which she told herself were beyond her control, Celia took her scrubbing equipment back to the kitchen and dumped it in the sink before running upstairs. There would always be time when she returned. Come to think of it, it might be a good idea to meet Mr Ryland and have everything out with him. With the air cleared perhaps she wouldn't find herself bursting into tears about things like a shabby house, which really didn't matter at all!

In her bedroom she quickly opened her largest case, still unpacked, and found what she looked for immediately. It was a smart, ultra-fashionable model, in a beautiful fine silk jersey, guaranteed to imbue its wearer with confidence as well as style. Relieved, she lifted it out and laid it across the bed. She recalled looking at it in London and considering it too smart to need up here. She couldn't actually remember doing so, but she must have changed her mind and put it in. Today it would act as a sort of armour against a man she disliked, a means of proving to him that, unlike Robin and Lucy, she was quite capable of standing on her own two feet.

She still had almost an hour, which gave her plenty of time to dress slowly and apply make-up with more attention to detail than she usually allowed. Her long tawny hair she brushed until it shone, and tied it back from her face in a sophisticated chignon which emphasised the dazzling beauty of her eyes, the ridiculous length of her lashes darkened by two applications of the mascara she normally used only for work. It seemed imperative that she hide her growing nervousness behind a cloak of ambiguity, and her reflection in the glass when she finished showed someone completely different from the tear-stained, slightly grubby girl who had answered the telephone earlier.

It was exactly one o'clock when she heard his car outside and the shaky feeling inside her began again. It wasn't an actual physical trembling, but a peculiar weakness which at the very approach of the man seemed to attack her limbs, and this headlong plunge into contact with him only served to make these feelings worse. Not even the time and care she had taken over her appearance to secure an impervious front seemed to help her now. With a helpless sigh, Celia flung a fluffy fur jacket around her shoulders and ran down.

Quickly, before she could change her mind, she closed the door behind her and walked gracefully towards the car. To her surprise she saw it was chauffeur-driven, and Guy Ryland reclined in the back. He didn't attempt to get out, but his man did. He sat waiting while she slid in beside him, his cool gaze appraising on her smoothly groomed beauty.

'Well worth the waiting for,' he said suavely.

'Surely,' she retorted sharply, with a pointed glance towards the chaffeur, 'I don't warrant this V.I.P. treatment?' If her greeting seemed less gracious than his it was more than he deserved that she should speak to him at all, she excused herself.

His eyes glinted as he flicked a rug across her knees, his action, she thought, deliberately careless. 'A driver around here is a necessity rather than a luxury,' he grunted, his eyes, not quite so casual as his words, on her lightly flushed cheeks. 'He saves me hours of time.'

His deep voice, mercilessly attractive, cut through her newly achieved composure as she attempted to nod in a disinterested fashion. It was like plunging head-first into the sea, this first magnetic contact, a baptism of fire followed by water, more devastating than the flames it failed to put out. She was too aware of his dark-suited elegance, the slight swarthiness to his complexion which gave him the slightly foreign look which women might find exciting or frightening, according to individual taste. Celia tried to convince herself, as she stared away from him, that she found him neither.

'Do you usually think in depth?' he queried, his eyes mocking as he regarded her.

'Perhaps you intentionally set out to give me food for thought,' she shrugged, pretending to concentrate on the traffic-jammed streets as they moved towards the centre of the city. 'You ask me out, knowing well how we dislike each other. You insist I spend Christmas in your house knowing perfectly well we have nothing to say to each

44

other. It makes one believe that hate might be just as tenacious as love.'

'Certainly,' he said softly, 'neither emotion thrives on neglect.'

'But of the two, hate could have the deeper roots.' Beneath his sardonic gaze she was unhappily conscious that her brief observation sounded slightly naïve.

'Especially when watered by a too persistent memory,' he quipped, his dark brows derisive. 'Come, Miss Kingsley, we could continue indefinitely. One shouldn't be so prosaic. If you've continued to hate me during all this time then perhaps I should feel flattered, but I can assure you the hate is all on your side.'

'Only because you deliberately provoked it,' she flung at him, admitting dispassionately that which otherwise she might have sought to hide. His cool indifference destroyed her own attempts to achieve just that. His arrant amusement, seeking and finding each sensitive nerve of her being, aroused some kind of inner turmoil impossible to define properly.

His eyes glittered as he leaned nearer. 'Merely by what I did three years ago?' Lightly he raised his hand towards the great department stores of Market Street. 'By buying something which only my money could save I'm condemned for ever as a rogue. How does a man defend his own actions, Miss Kingsley, against a girl who has already judged him? I hope I shouldn't be foolish enough to try.'

'I shouldn't be foolish enough to listen!'

'But there are other ways, Miss Kingsley, that a man might confound those who seek to disparage him. It's not always the woman who seeks a subtle revenge.'

Celia had a crazy notion that he was threatening her and unconsciously shrank back into her corner, but perhaps she was being stupid. If he was speaking from a personal angle it could only be because of his arrogant male pride. He had never been in danger of losing anything else. And he surely wouldn't have the nerve to accuse her of having a long

45

memory if he was guilty of the same thing himself! She glanced at him uncertainly. How could one tell? He relaxed, lazily indolent, against the luxurious upholstery, yet there lurked in his eyes the look of the tiger ready to spring.

Swiftly she said, 'You still haven't told me why you've asked me out. Now that I'm here I'm beginning to suspect I've allowed myself to be stampeded into a lot of unnecessary trouble. Was it really something we couldn't have discussed over the phone?'

'Never mind—for the moment,' he commanded. 'I dislike discussing anything immediately before a meal. Be patient, we're almost there. I thought you'd be too busy renewing your acquaintance with your home town to want to talk about anything else.'

'It hasn't changed, not that I've noticed, and I have been glancing through the window,' she informed him dryly, unable to believe that this was the real reason for his silence. She inclined her head to where a towering office block dominated the city centre. 'We had the multi-storey before I left, and unless they've replaced the Central Library and our Gothic-style Town Hall, I can't see very much difference. Perhaps the Canal has run dry?'

His bold, sculptured mouth quirked at one corner, but he said firmly, 'Such flippancy doesn't become you, Miss Kingsley, after an absence of almost three years. We mustn't leave you with the impression that time has stood still, but that can wait until another day.'

Not entirely sure what he meant, she didn't ask, declaring to herself that she wasn't interested in whatever he had in mind. The sooner this little outing was over and she was on her way home the better she would be pleased! She lay back, trying rather desperately to emulate his ease of manner, and sought refuge in silence until they arrived swiftly at the restaurant of his choice.

The restaurant was one of the smartest and most expensive in town and the service matched it. They didn't have a secluded table but one of the most obvious on the floor. Because of her training Celia wasn't really conscious that she attracted some attention. That she had been taught to wear clothes which showed to best advantage her thin, seductive figure was, she considered, part of the job. Never was she fully aware of her own attractiveness, and she would have been surprised to know that the man beside her was. His keen eye had noticed the unconcealed curiosity and interest of other diners, and he was quite content that it should be so. For his own hard, masculine good looks, Celia's glowing, youthful beauty proved the perfect foil.

He gave her an excellent lunch, but to her surprise made no attempt to linger or even to talk very much. He was attentive, watching her throughout the meal, but his manner was enigmatically remote. There was nothing at all to indicate that he had anything of paramount importance to say.

The hors d'oeuvres were followed by the finest fillets of steak, and there was wine and black coffee with brown sugar and cream. Not for a long time could Celia remember feeling so ravenous, yet somehow she was only able to nibble.

'You surely don't need to be frugal, not with your figure,' Guy said dryly, destroying the soothing silence with his unerring personal touch. Immediately she felt the weight of his glance sweeping over her, resting lightly on her scarcely touched plate.

'I do feel hungry,' to her surprise she found herself confessing with some bewilderment, 'but I can't seem to manage more than a little. You must excuse me.' The last she tacked on, suddenly realising what she was saying, and made her apology stiff, not wishing him to imagine that she was indulging in any form of self-pity.

A smile flickered momentarily in his eyes. 'Perhaps this is all proving a little too much for you,' he mused. 'Too much to assimilate too soon. Is it your family or myself, or just things in general, I wonder?' Then before she could find words to protest he waved abruptly for the bill. 'Come,' he said firmly, as they left the restaurant, 'we must find

47

somewhere quieter and try to sort everything out.'

Outside the day had grown even colder, but the interior heating system of the car was such that within a few minutes she was beautifully warm. The door closed and Celia was again aware of Guy Ryland beside her, and could feel the nervous beating of her heart as the car swung swiftly through the city streets, taking them steadily towards the suburbs on the outer reaches of the town.

They had gone several miles before she broke the silence between them. 'Where are we going?' she asked, suddenly startled to realise that they were not travelling in a home-ward direction.

'Wait and see,' he returned enigmatically, not obviously moved by the pale apprehension on her face. 'You won't regret the short journey, that's all I'm going to tell you.'

Celia was beginning to feel like a chess-piece which he moved according to the dictates of his whim. Foolish might not be the exact word to describe how she felt, but it would be near enough to serve. 'I would rather go straight home, if you don't mind,' she exclaimed.

'Why?' his tone was patently mocking. 'You can have nothing there that calls for any great urgency. I should advise you to forget about it while you can.'

She was quick to read between the lines, to realise that he understood only too well how the general atmosphere of the house had deteriorated almost visibly from neglect. But she refused to be drawn into open criticism of her family, holding him more directly responsible himself. Hadn't he taken the house from them in the first place, leaving them only tenants' rights? And, as if this hadn't been enough, the confiscation of their much-loved Mrs Timpson proved indisputably his intention to lower their living standards even further. Uneasily she sought to disclaim any personal responsibility. Surely he was much too successful to allow one slap, given in a moment of anger, to drive him to such lengths? After all, any depletion of their circumstances would rebound only on Robin and Lucy.

This she intended having out with him before the day was much older, but if he could wait then so could she. It was not impossible that she might lose her temper and was reluctant to provide entertainment for a curious chauffeur.

She became aware of Guy Ryland's waiting silence and murmured the first thing to enter her head—something vague about promising to have dinner ready, and having shopping to do. He merely shrugged, making no audible reply, but his eyes, flickering over her coolly, implied quite clearly that a girl like herself shouldn't have cooking to do at all.

It was a new experience to be treated to such tangible disapproval and Celia wished, not for the first time, that he had been driving. Sitting here with him she felt too close. His arm brushed her shoulder at each turn of the road, and when he looked down on her and spoke she could almost feel his breath on her cheek. It seemed he derived a certain satisfaction from making sure that she was aware of him.

He disturbed the remote aura of detachment which she had built up carefully over the past years, and she liked him none the better for it. With the air of one deliberately kidnapped against her will she stared from the window again, watching blindly as they left Manchester behind and approached the open country. It was still fairly early in the afternoon, yet already the light appeared to be fading, shrouding every landmark in industrial gloom and making it increasingly difficult to tell exactly where they were going. They crawled carefully through some village before she recognised it as being near the Forest of Rossendale, a particularly unspoilt area on the moors. Here she remembered being before, although none of it appeared very familiar. She did know that they were some considerable distance from Manchester, and curiosity mixed briefly with alarm. This man might be her brother's employer, but what did she really know about him? She hadn't even had the sense to mention to anyone that she was having lunch with him. If she was to regret this peculiar outing then she could only blame herself.

Her feelings of apprehension growing, she was about to order him to stop, to take her straight back, when they turned in to a narrow drive and within seconds swept to a stop before a large house. It was completely secluded by trees and Celia had not noticed it from the roadway, but she saw now that it was a house of some size, old and well cared for, set like a gem amidst a swath of wide lawns, noticeably green, even at this time of the year. It was stone-built and immaculate in the classical tradition of the seventeenth-century, but beautiful in its own right, possessing all the elegance and solidarity of that particular decade. For one long, suspended moment Celia felt more than a twinge of envy in her heart as she stared entranced.

Her breath caught, but before she could speak to ask Guy Ryland who lived there, he was out, not waiting for his man to precede him, his steps lithe as he came around to open her door.

'Here we are,' he said, his hand firm beneath her arm as he turned her towards the entrance, a faint flicker of satisfaction lighting his dark eyes as they rested on her enchanted face. 'I thought,' he murmured in her ear, 'you might like where I live.'

Swiftly she controlled her too expressive features. 'Why, yes, why shouldn't I?' She tried to speak coolly.

'The house but not the man, eh? He's something quite different?' Guy Ryland's voice came dryly as he read her thoughts with devious accuracy.

Colour flared delicately in her cold cheeks as she swung indignantly around to him. 'Why have you brought me here?' she countered wildly. 'Robin told me you lived in Manchester.'

He didn't reply immediately, but turned and spoke to the man behind him, dismissing him for a while. 'Come along,' he said, again taking Celia's arm, ignoring the fact that only a minute ago she had almost wrenched it from his grasp, 'it's much too cold to stand around out here. Robin is quite right,' he added, 'I do have a place in Manchester, as well as other towns, but Cheverly is my real home.'

Cheverly! Even the name could not be faulted. It was a lovely house, and if, like her father's shop, it had fallen into the wrong hands, it would be foolish to pretend that because of this she disliked it. In confessing to be fond of it Guy Ryland did, at least, prove himself to be a man of some discernment.

Unable to resist a desire to have a glimpse of the interior, Celia let herself be drawn inside. As in the car, she was too conscious of his nearness, which seemed to render a certain numbness to her intelligence. She was through the door before she could find words to protest, and almost immediately found herself confronted by Mrs Timpson.

'Why, Timmy!' she gasped, no less astonished than the woman herself. It hadn't occurred to her for one moment that Mrs Timpson would be here. She had imagined her installed in one of the best suburbs of Manchester, and had postponed asking Robin for her address as she had felt reluctant to visit her for fear of meeting Guy Ryland. Now here was Timmy, holding out both hands, not trying to hide how delighted she was to see her. 'This is wonderful, Timmy,' Celia heard herself exclaiming eagerly, 'I never expected to find you here.'

'You can borrow her for half an hour, Mrs Timpson,' Guy Ryland broke in abruptly, apparently having no wish to share in such obvious sentimentality, 'then bring her to the library.'

Quite willingly this time, Celia followed Mrs Timpson through to her own domain, a small but comfortable sitting-room beside the kitchen. 'I've missed you, Timmy,' Celia confessed, after refusing the offer of coffee. 'If we're only to be allowed half an hour, let's make the most of it,' she added.

There was so much to talk about, so much bound up with

51

those early days of childhood when Mrs Timpson's warm sympathy had dried up many a childish tear. 'I'm ashamed I didn't return regularly to see you,' Celia said, her eyes brooding, 'then much of this might have been avoided.'

Mrs Timpson didn't pretend not to understand. 'It wasn't your fault I left, dear.'

'But if I'd stayed—among the three of us we surely could have afforded enough to keep you.' Celia knew she spoke bluntly, but Timmy had always encouraged them to speak their minds, with her at any rate.

Mrs Timpson smiled, confirming Celia's opinion that she wouldn't be offended by a little frankness, although she did say reprovingly, 'It's wrong that you should think I left because of money.'

'But ...'

Momentarily the woman hesitated, her eyes affectionately drawn to Celia's anxious young face. 'If you must insist on the truth, dear, I didn't think I was needed any more. Robin and Lucy very rarely appeared for meals. They began using the house more as a place to sleep in. I don't think it was that they couldn't afford me, as you put it—although, mind you, I have no idea what Mr Guy pays them. I just had the impression that my presence was beginning to irritate them in some way.'

Celia stared at her with some bewilderment. 'But where did they go each evening if not home?'

'Out, I suppose, with friends. With their gregarious natures they both have plenty, though I'm not sure they were always the right kind. Lucy, you know, was never like you, Celia. You were the one who liked staying by the fire of an evening, the one who treated the house like a home. Even as a teenager, you must remember, Miss Lucy could scarcely bear to stay in. But for you, I used to think, your father would have been a very lonely man.'

And she had gone while he must have still needed her, when perhaps they had all needed her. 'If only I'd been there!' Regret tore the words from Celia, spreading an ache through her entire being. 'Aunt Mary never really needed me. She has at least three close friends who beg her annually to go and live with them. I like to pretend otherwise, but I believe she only stays in London because of me. I should have stayed,' she tacked on abruptly, feeling not far from tears.

'It wouldn't have made much difference, I don't think,' Mrs Timpson hastened to assure her, with a shrewd glance at Celia's tense face. 'Mr Guy did all he could.'

Celia ignored this. 'How did you ever come to work for him?' she exclaimed, unable to restrain a note of disapproval. 'I know I'm here with him today,' she admitted frankly, 'but I don't like him.'

Mrs Timpson sighed, a little alarmed. 'I shouldn't advise you to tell him this, dear, for your own sake, not mine. It's just a small hint, you always did have too much spirit, and I believe he prefers his—er—friends to be more subdued.'

Women friends, Timmy had meant! The hesitation didn't escape Celia for a second. 'But I don't happen to be one of his particular friends, Timmy. If you're curious, I'm only with him this afternoon because there are things he wants to discuss. I promise, if it's so important, to be discreet. I was merely curious to know how he persuaded you into his employment.'

Again Mrs Timpson didn't answer directly, but continued to regard Celia, frowning. 'To tell you the truth, Celia, I had no idea you knew him. You always avoided him because he was involved with the shop.'

'I did meet him once,' Celia volunteered guardedly.

'Oh, I see.' Apparently willing to leave it at that, Mrs Timpson nodded. 'Well, going back to your question. He called one evening, a few months after your father died, to see Robin. I'm afraid I was upset. I'd prepared a good dinner for Robin and Miss Lucy and neither of them had turned up or even bothered to give me a ring. So, to cut a long story short, Mr Guy sat down and shared it with me,

53

and was so taken with my cooking that he offered me a job, there and then!'

'And you took it right away?'

'Not straight away!' Mrs Timpson looked slightly hurt for the first time. 'I did talk it over with your brother and sister next day.'

'And ...?'

'I'm afraid I took them by surprise, putting it to them bluntly. They were unable to conceal that the prospect of being rid of me was pleasing.'

'Pleasing!' gasped Celia.

'Well, you see, dear,' Mrs Timpson smiled ruefully but without a trace of resentment, 'I think I was becoming a bit of an embarrassment. Not exactly a servant, nor one of the family. I suppose I was more like a poor relation who had outstayed her welcome, but they were too kind-hearted to say so outright. Anyway, it seemed they considered Mr Guy, or rather, his mother, to be the perfect solution. They liked to pretend Mr Guy was too important to offend.'

'I didn't think Mr Ryland had a mother,' Celia remarked.

'We all have, dear, but I know what you mean. She was a charming old lady. Not really so very old, come to that.'

'Was?'

'Yes, dear, she died very suddenly a few months ago, during the summer. She lived here. Mr Guy wasn't here a lot, but he did stay whenever he could, and when he had to be away he rang every day.'

'I see.' This news came as a surprise and threw Celia into some confusion, acquainting her as it did with a side of Guy Ryland she had never suspected. She said uncertainly, 'I suppose you know that Robin and Lucy are invited here for Christmas?'

Mrs Timpson nodded. 'At least,' she pondered, 'I think I remember Mr Guy saying something about it. Mrs Ryland's sister always came for Christmas, and Mr Guy thought one or two young people would provide a bit of company, so to speak. If his aunt hadn't been coming I

54

don't think he would have stayed at all, but he didn't want to disappoint her.'

Celia frowned, commenting dryly, 'Somehow I can't see him as a man prepared to go to such lengths to placate an elderly relation, no matter how fond of her he might be.'

'No—well,' Mrs Timpson's own brow creased slightly, as if the thought had also occurred to her, but it was also quite clear where her loyalties now lay, as she was obviously unwilling to discuss it. 'Anyway,' she went on, 'I've prepared rooms for half a dozen. We've plenty to spare, and Mr Guy is getting extra help for me in the kitchen.'

Celia digested this in silence. Timmy's enthusiasm was all a bit beyond her. 'But surely,' she asked, 'you don't intend staying on here now that Mrs Ryland has gone?'

'Why not? Mr Guy will be using the house just the same, and he needs someone to keep an eye on the place while he's away. Why not me?'

'No reason.' Reluctantly Celia rose to her feet as the bell rang, hating to be reminded in such a dominant fashion that her half-hour was up. 'As I told you, I just don't care for him, but I can certainly appreciate your point of view. You've settled in here and have every comfort.' Not even for Timmy's sake could she restrain that final note of bitterness.

When Timmy showed her into the library, Guy said crisply, 'Bring some tea, Mrs Timpson, with plenty of hot buttered toast. Miss Kingsley ate very little lunch.'

'Well,' he drawled, as the door closed behind Mrs Timpson and he moved to remove Celia's coat, 'what's the verdict?'

'If you mean Timmy,' Celia flinched, trying desperately to concentrate as his fingers caught her bare nape, 'if you mean Timmy,' she repeated, flushing, 'she seems happy enough.'

'Such a begrudging concession,' he said, with some asperity, flinging her coat across the back of a chair with one hand and catching hold of her arm with the other.

'Come nearer to the fire,' he commanded, thrusting her almost forcibly forward as she held back.

'I'm not cold.' Celia spoke swiftly, hating the way in which her heart jerked at his touch, but she sat down. Rather this than submit to being thrown into a chair physically, something which at this moment he looked quite capable of doing. 'I suppose,' she said faintly as a million shivers ran down her spine, 'Mrs Timpson was the reason you brought me here?'

'One of the reasons,' he corrected, 'and you must admit that if I hadn't more or less kidnapped you, you wouldn't have come on your own accord.'

'Possibly not,' she agreed coldly, feeling suddenly too weary to argue. This man's vitality exhausted her. There was about him a boundless, if restrained, energy which seemed to burn through her frailly erected defences, leaving her too vulnerable. Rather helplessly she lay back, and momentarily closed her wide blue eyes against his disturbingly masculine image, her pale creamy face utterly still. 'I still wish I hadn't come, though,' she added with visible effort, glancing up at him again.

She found his dark eyes intent upon her, but he merely shrugged his broad shoulders. His voice was full of hard irony. 'You enjoy hurting yourself, don't you, Celia? You're just as determined as ever to fight me every inch of the way.'

'You dislike opposition,' she retorted very quickly, refusing to retreat but finding the effort almost intolerable. 'I wasn't aware that you had any particular goal in mind.'

He ignored this as if she had never spoken. 'Your bruises wouldn't show so much if you gave in gracefully,' he said suavely, his eyes on her mouth.

Her skin tightened electrically, the underlying context of his words not clear, but spearing with a pointed deliberation through her body. It created a diversion for which she was grateful when Timmy returned with their tea.

She accepted the cup he poured out but refused toast

56

until he placed some on her plate. 'You're much too thin.' His eyes went slowly over her as he drank his own tea, until she flushed beneath his mocking gaze and protested, 'I'm not, really. My present job demands I should be slim, but I certainly don't starve myself.'

Defiantly she stared into his face, not knowing why she should be trying to explain herself. Just as she wasn't sure why, as he pointed out, she felt it necessary to fight him. It wasn't logical, she supposed, that the violent dislike she had known three years ago should still consume her so actively. She really had no great desire to either like him or not. All she wanted to do, if he would let her, was to forget him completely.

He was saying, 'This job of yours—I gather you're extremely successful?'

'Moderately so.' Quickly she looked away from him, not willing to talk about herself.

She might have known he thrived on opposition. 'You went as a management trainee, and now you model clothes?'

'Only during the seasonal shows, Mr Ryland.'

'An unusual mixture.'

'Perhaps. In between sessions I do work in the department and do a little outside for other firms. Not very much.'

'And you lost interest in the management side?'

She shook her head. 'You forget, Mr Ryland, that my position when I worked for my father was rather different. My main objective was to help him as much as possible, and after you took over this was no longer necessary. In London I felt in need of a complete change which, I'm sure you will agree, wasn't so surprising.'

'And the manager, as an old friend of your father's, quite understood,' Guy Ryland observed smoothly.

It wasn't a question but more of a statement, almost as if he had known. Which wasn't, of course, logical. 'Actually,' she said shortly, 'it was he who suggested I should try fashions in the first place.'

'And now he's about to retire, how will you fare?'

'Really, Mr Ryland,' Celia looked at him with open contempt, 'I see very little of him as it is. I might have taken his advice to begin with, but my recent success I've achieved entirely through my own efforts, not through favours from management.'

He took no notice of her indignation, treating it as he would an irritating fly, brushing it aside. 'You intend going to Bermuda. You've quite made up your mind?'

Not until later did it occur to Celia that he seemed to know a lot about her movements, more than she had divulged to either Robin or Lucy. Enough to make her wonder where he had acquired his information, and why she hadn't asked him at the time. Right now, coherent thought was shattered by his quick-fire questions, the glinting, assessing eyes, the arrogant curve to nostril and mouth. 'After the New Year,' she replied, as calmly as she could.

'I see.' Distantly he drawled the words, as if such an announcement was not to be taken seriously. 'I have,' he went on slowly, 'a proposition to put to you which you might find interesting. How would you like to return to Manchester and work for me?'

'For you!' Her face expressed disbelief that he should waste his time over such a proposal. She didn't even bother to eject a brief thank you. She merely added, 'No, I shouldn't like that at all.'

'Celia,' he leaned back in his chair, stretching his long, well-shaped limbs to the fire, surveying her dryly, 'no girl in her right senses refuses, and keeps on refusing, merely because it's become a kind of habit. You have to come around to my way of thinking sooner or later, you know that.'

'I know nothing of the sort.' Celia's tawny head spun as her spine tautened defensively. Why did there seem a double meaning to so many things he said? 'Fortunately I don't consider I owe you a thing, Mr Ryland, even if there

58

are others in my family who imagine they're indebted to you.'

'And still are, my dear Celia, and don't you forget it.'

At his tone of voice, Celia felt herself go positively hot and cold, the recurring, irresistible longing to slap that dark face almost overcoming her. 'My brother,' she spluttered furiously, 'is supposed to be your manager, in charge of a large department store. Surely, after three years of hard work you can't say he hasn't more than repaid anything that might be owing?'

Guy Ryland laughed, but to Celia his laughter was too calculating to hold any real mirth. His glance caught hers and held it as he replied with what appeared to be deliberate emphasis. 'Your brother, Celia, does manage, but without any apparent method, or at least none which he appears to using successfully. It's not obvious that he has any original ideas in that very pleasant head of his, and the annual turnover is less than it was three years ago. And don't start protesting that you can't believe it. I never make rash statements, certainly never without the relevant figures to back me up.'

'Then why retain him any longer?' Celia, clinging rather desperately to the notion that Guy Ryland might be bluffing, decided vaguely to challenge him. He might have nothing very concrete to go on. He might only be trying to frighten her for some perverse reason of his own.

'It suited me.' Guy Ryland's broad shoulders flexed indifferently. 'I have plenty of other business to attend to and he kept things ticking over. I probably have myself to blame. I've been too busy to stop and take a good look, but certain things recently have been brought to my notice.'

'Such as?' Celia heard herself whispering through lips grown coldly stiff. Had this man brought her all the way here to tell her that Robin had been up to something criminal? Her breath caught painfully in her throat as she waited for his answer.

59

CHAPTER FOUR

FOR what seemed an inordinate length of time Guy Ryland's silvery glance licked over the silent girl, the distress in her face evidently more to his liking than her previous imperviousness. He saw how she sat with her hands clenched and how her small, white teeth bit into her soft bottom lip. It was an oddly nervous, uncertain gesture, entirely at odds with her sleek appearance, and his own lips quirked at the corners before he spoke.

'I'm sure, Celia, that a discussion on the extent of your brother's shortcomings would do little to help our somewhat strained relations. I've been pointing out one or two innovations that he might try. One was that he should update his fashion departments. Some of the models I noticed appeared to be decades behind times. It was a thought that you might be of considerable assistance to him in achieving a sort of minor revolution.'

Celia felt her heartbeats slow to a more normal throb. If this was the worst of Robin's transgressions then she might feel justified in breathing again. She forced herself to go carefully. 'How could I help?'

'A change of policy such as I have in mind might be more acceptable from someone with your experience.'

'Meaning that there would be considerable opposition?'

'Nothing you couldn't overcome, with my help and your own impeccable good taste. New ideas are not easily instilled in heads not willing to accept them, but I should have thought it a challenge worth considering.'

Momentarily, in spite of her prevailing antipathy, Celia felt tempted. In her teens she remembered noticing that many of the clothing departments were old-fashioned. She even recalled pointing it out to her father, who hadn't been prepared to listen, clinging as he had to his outmoded belief that women wished only for good cut and durability, material which would wear for years. He had refused to accept that while both these things were still necessary to a certain extent, there was a growing demand for something cheaper and more trendy, more easily discarded at the end of each season. That Robin had allowed this state of affairs to continue surprised her to the point of almost doubting the truth of what Guy Ryland said.

She heard him adding persuasively, obviously mistaking her silence for acquiescence, 'You could have a free hand. Some of the staff Robin retains appear to be almost of pensionable age, if not past it. A few suitable redundancies might not come amiss.'

'Why, how dare you suggest such a thing?' she cried, resentment which she knew to be childish flaring. 'Many of these people whom you so disparagingly refer to have been with the firm since they left school.'

'Which might have been at the beginning of the century, judging from the appearance of some of them,' he grunted dryly. 'Certainly I'm not exaggerating, and a business doesn't thrive on sentiment, Celia.'

Celia felt positively choked as she glared at him. 'I think I'd rather lose money than make it by throwing people out on to the streets! What would you condemn some of these women to? Several have devoted their whole lives to the store. They haven't married—what would their retirement be? A two-roomed flat in a high rise block or an old tenement, with nothing to look at all day but four walls!'

He regarded her, his firm mouth tightening with a natural impatience. 'I did not, Celia, as you so wildly imply, suggest we throw people into the streets. And if you must theorise, how about the thousands of youngsters who can't even get a start? They sit at home or wander the town all day, a way of life which eventually knocks most of the incentive out of them. There are so many ways of looking

61

at this situation, my dear, and no very easy answer to much of it. But I do know this, that unless something is done within a very short time, Kingsley's Department Store will not be open to employ anyone, young or old.'

'But you wouldn't let things go as far as that, Mr Ryland, would you? Not with your business acumen.' Celia's tones, despite her efforts to strive for indifference, were edged with satire.

She might have known that his own caustic wit would be more than a match for hers. He retorted coolly, 'A wise man never sticks with a sinking ship. And don't forget that while I have more than enough to keep me busy elsewhere, your brother might never survive. Reputations have an unfortunate habit of clinging to people.'

Celia flinched, eyes sparkling with anger at his audacity. 'Robin might not be the only one to be affected by the failure of the store. It could also reflect on you, and with good reason. Men like you who take on more than they can reasonably cope with ask for all they get.'

Again the corners of his mouth quirked, but whether this time with amusement or annoyance she couldn't make out. With a quick glance at the gathering darkness he rose lithely to his feet. 'You interest me, Celia, as does your whole family. Robin meanders as if tomorrow and its repercussions didn't exist. Lucy is a sharp little go-getter in an entirely different direction. But you, I think, my dear Celia, are the conundrum I have yet to solve.'

'Why bother, Mr Ryland?' Celia was on her own feet, a clear hint, she hoped, that she was more than ready to go if this was what he had in mind. Bitterly she realised the futility of attacking him further. Possibly she would only succeed in making a fool of herself by letting him drive her to further stupid remarks. His own about Lucy filled her with renewed chill.

He said briefly as he reached for her coat and draped it calmly around her tense shoulders, his hands lingering deliberately where he drew the lapels beneath her chin, 'I think we'll leave that question for the moment. I have an appointment which unfortunately I must keep. You might like to say goodbye to Mrs Timpson while I ring for the car.'

Later, returning to Manchester, Celia had a feeling that she was on a sort of switchback, and was exhausted by efforts which had achieved precisely nothing. Guy Ryland, apparently with other things on his mind, scarcely spoke, and while she welcomed his silence she found nothing comforting in it. Again she was overcome by the impression of a leopard watching its prey, ready to pounce.

Nearing the city, she was startled when in the darkness of the car, he suddenly reached over and took her hand—a surprisingly unpredictable gesture which drove the breath from her body. She tried to draw back like a wild creature sensing a trap, the now familiar tremors rushing through her at the feel of his firm, lean fingers holding hers. 'You could try calling me Guy,' he suggested softly, his grip tightening as she strove to pull away, 'It could be easier in future.'

'As there won't be any for us,' she choked. 'I can't see that it matters, Mr Ryland!' His name she contrived somehow to bring out with burning emphasis.

There was one awful moment when his fingers hurt before he almost threw her hand back into her lap, his short exclamation derisive. 'As you like, Celia my dear. If this is the way you want it. It makes little difference to me —it will all be the same in the end.'

The colossal nerve of the man, she thought afterwards. Had he imagined she would be bewitched, finding him utterly irresistible, when she only knew an urgent desire to evade him? Her reactions to the avalanche of feeling that swept through her whenever he touched her, she ignored. All the same, unable to suppress a normal feminine curiosity, she wondered what he meant when he talked of the end. It was almost as though he had mapped out a campaign, with victory for himself a foregone conclusion!

63

Unfortunately the cold atmosphere of the house in Moor-land Road did nothing to cheer her, and as she ran up-stairs she couldn't help but compare it with the one she had just left. Before she left, Mrs Timpson had taken her up-stairs at Cheverly, and everywhere had been an air of under-stated luxury. The bathroom into which she had been shown had been a dream of white and gold, deeply carpeted, the walls lined extravagantly with mirrors in which her un-consciously wistful face had been reflected too readably. How was it, she wondered vaguely, that her father, though owning a sizeable establishment, had never seemed able to live in even a remotely comparable style?

Moving listlessly, she removed her smart coat and dress, replacing them with a pair of more serviceable slacks and a sweater. She sighed as she hung the soft dress carefully away in her wardrobe, regretting the obvious necessity to take it off while realising how unsuitable it would be for such mundane tasks as lighting fires and preparing an even-ing meal. Half enviously, she tried to keep her thoughts from straying to Guy Ryland's opulent lounge, picturing him enjoying a pre-dinner drink in pleasurable anticipation of Mrs Timpson's cooking. The woman he invited to share all that would scarcely be called upon to lift so much as a finger!

Lucy didn't come in. She rang instead, explaining sweetly over the telephone that she had been invited out to something special she couldn't refuse. Robin, when he ar-rived, didn't appear surprised.

'She seldom comes home after work,' he told an indig-nant Celia. 'Usually she freshens up in my office before going off somewhere. Sometimes I think she keeps a more extensive wardrobe there than here.'

'But my first proper evening home—actually, my second,' Celia wailed, feeling hurt and not bothering to hide it.

Robin grinned, but ruefully, adopting the role of peace-maker. 'Well, you know, Celia, how it is. After you deserted us for almost three years it's rather difficult to put the clock back. She hasn't had you to consider, and, being Lucy, she isn't going to start now. Not right away.'

'Has she gone out with Denis Ryland?' Celia asked with a little moue of distaste.

'I believe so,' Robin shrugged. 'I had thought we might discuss this rationally among the three of us, but it's almost as if she's suspicious and intent on keeping out of the way.'

'And I had imagined her still as a sort of half-child, waiting to be tucked up in bed, eager for advice.'

He laughed, 'That, Celia, is a mental distortion. Lucy was never like that, not even as a child, not so that I can remember. She's much older than you are in everything but actual years.'

Uneasily Celia recalled Guy Ryland's slightly derogatory remarks. Surely Lucy wasn't really like this? Robin—and Guy—could be mistaken. Whatever happened she mustn't allow herself to condemn Lucy out of hand purely because of an entirely masculine viewpoint. Lucy, like herself, might have found it necessary to wear some sort of armour as a defence against the world in general. People often regarded the too vulnerable with a pitying kind of contempt. During the next few days Celia vowed she would discover the real truth.

In the meantime it proved a welcome, if regrettable, diversion to be able to mention to Robin that she had been taken by Guy Ryland to see Timmy. 'So it's perhaps just as well,' she added wryly, 'that Lucy has decided to stay out, as I have nothing prepared.'

Robin whistled and glanced at her quickly, his mild amazement mixed with more than a little respect. 'You don't say!' he exclaimed. 'You must, in spite of your wasp-ish attitude, have made quite an impression.'

'I think he was thinking of Timmy,' Celia retorted swiftly, not adding that Guy had also taken her for lunch, or anything of their conversation concerning the shop.

'You could be right,' Robin agreed, although obviously not as willing as she had thought to be misled. 'Guy Ryland usually thinks mainly of himself, but I might be wrong to wonder if Timmy was all he had in mind. I suppose only time will tell—and it doesn't really matter about dinner.'

Eventually, after some discussion about it, she and Robin went out and ate a light meal in a nearby café. It wasn't opulent or even very satisfying, but it was convenient and comfortable. They didn't dress, and comparing her well-cut but ordinary slacks with the ritzy outfit she had worn for lunch, Celia sighed grimly. With Guy Ryland one would never dare appear dressed thus. This she seemed to know instinctively, and she shuddered for no apparent reason at all.

On the following day, deciding to ignore the house for a few hours, she went with Robin and Lucy to the store. Robin surprised her by being far from enthusiastic when, instead of beginning to gather up their breakfast dishes, she belted herself into an outdoor coat. Lucy, when Celia informed them as to where she was going, was downright sarcastic in trying to maintain there was no necessity for her to go with them at all.

'Well, just let me mention that I have presents to buy,' Celia said brightly, refusing to be disheartened by their suddenly glum faces. 'I see no reason why not. You surely don't expect me to spend the whole day here on my own?'

'Why not?' Lucy inquired sharply. 'You did come home to sort the house out—or so I thought?'

'And to prepare for Christmas,' Celia replied, now equally short, 'but I find I'll have to stock up with provisions. All you appear to have in the house is a packet of cornflakes and half a loaf of bread.'

'We don't eat here a lot,' they both chorused, on this one point at least entirely in agreement.

'Fine,' Celia shrugged, exasperated into momentary indifference, 'but we've Christmas to think about now,' she continued firmly, 'and little time to do it in.'

'Christmas!' Lucy screamed, adding all in one breath, 'I'm spending it at Cheverly, you can do what you like!'

'Lucy!' Robin's voice held with effort the faintest note of authority.

'I'm sorry, Celia,' Lucy muttered a grudging apology, her small face sullen. 'I don't want to quarrel but not even for you will I stay here, and I'd accepted before I had any idea you were coming.'

Even Robin, despite his disapproval of Lucy's slight hysteria, began to look wheedling. 'There's nothing much to keep us here, Celia, as I've already told you. And think of the expense. Guy Ryland doesn't believe in stinting things when he's in the mood. Besides, you could be putting us in an awkward position. I'm not sure he would take kindly to a refusal.'

Were they all, Celia wondered, scared of the man? Even Timmy seemed wary of annoying him. Crossly she regarded their anxiously apprehensive faces. 'You must do as you think best, of course, but don't expect me to join you.' If she kept on repeating it they might eventually believe her.

At the shop, as Guy Ryland had warned, she found few changes. The years, so full for her, had made little difference. Curiously she wandered through the large departments which at one time she had known so well, feeling the sharp, familiar ache of nostalgia returning. The conurbation of busy Manchester, sprawling widely on the Manchester Ship Canal, with its fifteenth-century cathedral, famous libraries and art galleries. With increasing interest she had explored the city as she'd grown older and more able to understand the unavoidable, but sometimes strange, blending of old and new. She had watched the old mill chimneys coming down, the slum clearance operations removing many of the derelict nineteenth-century factories and workers' houses. These, she recalled, had often been crammed chaotically together, but she wasn't sure if she liked any better the multi-storey buildings which so often took their place.

In London she had hoped emotionally to escape from it, yet how could one ever do that when one loved it, and was so proud of its magnificent past?

With a despairingly impatient shrug, Celia deliberately turned her thoughts away. She was too young, surely, to be thinking along these lines, to feel committed to a place by such tedious bonds. She would feel quite differently, come another day.

The shop wasn't really busy although it was almost Christmas when, she supposed, it should have been full. Some of the older staff even had time to recognise her and she spent longer than she had intended chatting to them, but throughout she didn't fail to notice that much of what Guy Ryland had talked about was true. The departments were extremely old-fashioned, the clothing housed mainly in the heavy mahogany cabinets which lined the walls, and the one or two models on display could well, she imagined despondently, have graced a museum. There was little she saw that she would be pleased to wear herself, and she was no teenager!

She tackled Robin about it later in his office. His secretary said he wasn't busy, that Celia could go in. It had been their father's office, and in some unexpected way it pleased her enormously to see Robin sitting there. Recalling Guy Ryland's displeasure at the state of the shop she couldn't suppress a small shudder of foreboding. How much longer could Robin hope to remain there if he didn't bestir himself?

'Why don't you try to expand a bit?' she began badly, trying, because she felt positively traitorous, to be extremely tactful but not succeeding. 'I mean,' she hurried on, as his welcoming smile faded, 'you could try stocking a variety of styles from different manufacturers. Something to cater for every age group. Shops within the shop, if you follow me? I expect it's called modernisation.'

'Modernisation?' Far from seeming annoyed, Robin chewed over the word slowly. 'I suppose,' he said wryly, 'you're comparing us with London. Well, I just haven't the time. I'm not even sure I have the inclination. Which isn't to say that I'm unaware of the present trend of catering chiefly for the younger set. But I just can't see my departments full of the weird type of garment you choose to describe as clothes.'

'Yet surely, Robin,' she argued, 'if it meant an increase in profits, wouldn't it be a good thing? And wouldn't it strengthen your own position with the firm?'

He frowned, 'I don't think I need worry about that!'

In turn, Celia's own brow creased as she stared at him. His complacency was disturbing. 'Could you—I mean, if you were to approach Mr Ryland would he be willing to provide the necessary funds for expansion?' She hadn't meant to go so far and prayed Robin wouldn't suspect that such an idea had been sown in her head by Guy Ryland himself in the first place.

'I daresay he might, but I have no wish to approach him, and I'd advise you to keep that elegant little nose of yours out of my business!' He spoke half crossly, and with, as she had feared, a slowly dawning comprehension, but before he could add more the door opened and Guy Ryland, unannounced, walked into the room. 'I had no idea,' Robin spoke distinctly, 'it was going to be this kind of morning!'

'I'm in town, as you know.' Deliberately Guy ignored the satire-laden tones of Robin's voice as his eyes swept over Celia, her flushed face apparently providing a note of interest. 'You're out early this morning, Miss Kingsley,' he added, his gaze lingering.

'She's Christmas shopping,' Robin explained, with exaggerated briefness, before Celia could reply herself. 'She's a very generous girl, my sister. Already she's been giving me the full benefit of her advice.'

Happily she could have slain Robin on the spot, especially as she fully realised that Guy Ryland was more than aware of what Robin was on about. Her pulse jerked as Guy came to stand beside her, and she felt her cheeks grow hot, in a way entirely at odds with her hard won sophistication. The last thing she wanted was to get involved with anything here. 'I'm sure,' she said lightly, 'Mr Ryland is in a hurry, Robin, and I really must be going.' Unconsciously she found herself edging backwards, only to find Guy obstructing the way. 'If you would excuse me, Mr Ryland,' she added pointedly, 'I wouldn't want to be a nuisance.'

But his hand went out as she turned to fly, holding her firmly to his side. Once again there was a wholly breathless moment as he looked lazily down at her, his eyes exploring her warmly tinted face. 'How very thoughtful of you, Celia,' he murmured conversationally. 'But don't worry, I'd really like you to stay. Robin's not the only one to appreciate a little advice. I think it's about time I started to really concentrate on this store. Three years ago, when this property first came on to the market, I bought it because I had it earmarked for future development. I hadn't any actual plans for it then.'

'But you'd already made my father two offers!' Celia exclaimed, for Robin's sake refraining from calling Guy Ryland a liar, but unable to let him get away with such a statement.

'I had?' His dark eyes narrowed coolly over her, but he said nothing more.

Celia couldn't be sure whether that had been a question or not. Glancing uncertainly at Robin she noticed he was clearly uncomfortable and decided to leave it. She could always do a little investigating on her own. She was fast learning the futility of attacking Guy Ryland about anything without having a complete set of facts to back her up. He could, she thought bitterly, twist the truth until one couldn't tell fact from fiction!

'I should like you both,' she heard him commanding softly, 'to accompany me on a tour of inspection. I'm sure you'll enjoy it. Afterwards, Robin, I hope your sister will agree to joining us for lunch.'

'Just to make sure your restaurant is up to standard, I expect,' she said frankly to Robin, Guy's dark arrogance making her eyes flash. It was a moment of panic when dignity deserted her, but she was overcome by a peculiar drowning sensation—of being swept along in a direction she would not voluntarily have taken. 'Anyway, I'm going home,' she spoke with a forced determination, 'I have plenty to keep me busy there.'

'Oh no, you don't!' Almost before she had finished speaking Guy's grasp on her arm tightened and he had whipped her through the door in seconds, his swift movements hard and masculine, utterly without mercy. 'If you refuse to co-operate,' he ground out, for once appearing on the verge of losing his temper, 'your brother won't sit in that chair much longer!'

'I've often envied those who can secure their own way by threats!' she choked.

'It's the only language you seem to understand, Miss Kingsley, although there are other methods I might try.'

His brief laughter enfolded her, and with an effort she jerked her arm free as, from the corner of her eye, she saw Robin following. 'You leave me with little other option,' she said scornfully, but she went quietly, not prepared to be seen being dragged along the corridor by Guy Ryland. Something she was quite sure he was capable of doing if he so chose!

Her glance stayed on Robin's downcast face. He and Lucy must be two of the most unfortunate people in the world to have this man for a boss. It was quite obvious from their unhappy expressions. In spite of what Robin said, Celia felt sure that Lucy hadn't always been so contrary. This situation, combined with a romance she must keep secret, could be stretching the poor girl's nerves to breaking point. Guy Ryland was so busy expanding his large textile empire that he didn't mind whom he trampled on, just so long as he got what he was after!

Perhaps it was time, Celia thought tensely, that he got more than he bargained for. Why should he be allowed to ravage and plunder other people's emotions? There must be a way of making him suffer, just as she seemed to be suffering at this moment from an overpowering and completely alien antagonism. It wasn't comfortable, nor was it sensible that when he touched her, as he seemed fond of doing, her senses should swim so weakly. No man could be completely indestructible, he must surely have a weak spot somewhere. Maybe it was up to her to find it. The idea persisted, provocatively, although there was no time then to consider it seriously, but while she thrust it impatiently to the back of her mind, it refused to be totally annihilated.

Their walk through the store occupied the remainder of the morning. They didn't see Lucy, as she worked in one of the offices and these they didn't go near. Chiefly Guy concentrated on the fashion departments, discussing what he had in mind. Before they had finished he had roughed out various improvements which to Celia's surprise didn't constitute a vast upheaval, although he warned that this would come.

'Within a year, or eighteen months, you won't know the place,' he said.

'After that time we might not want to,' Celia rejoined with a sugar-like sweetness.

They went in to lunch. 'I've offered your sister the job of helping to reorganise,' Guy said suavely, after they had ordered from the varied but rather ordinary menu. 'Didn't she tell you?' he inquired, with a traitorous grin.

'Good heavens, no!' Robin was startled and impressed but obviously put out as he turned to Celia. 'You never said anything.'

Annoyed, she felt her face flush again as she almost glared at Guy. 'Because I wasn't interested. In the job, I mean, so there wasn't much point. Besides,' she added sharply, 'Mr Ryland was just talking generally.'

'I'm not now,' he replied.

'Well, then . . .?' Robin's voice deepened with amazement as his brows rose like puzzled question marks.

'I'm still not interested.' Mutinously Celia shook her

silky head, inwardly furious that Robin should be so clearly questioning her sanity in passing up such an opportunity.

'Perhaps she'll change her mind. It is, after all, a woman's prerogative,' Guy murmured suavely, ostensibly in the role of a peacemaker.

Celia quivered, a pulse beating rapidly in her white throat as she tried to fathom the dry note in his voice, not caring for the chill swirl of premonition which suddenly hit her. 'I think this time you'll find yourself wrong, Mr Ryland,' she said tightly, her eyes intense. 'Bermuda, I've been told, has more to offer than Manchester in January.'

'I shouldn't believe it, if I were you.' He looked at her directly, his face full of hard vitality. He ignored Robin, who listened with interest to this surprising conversation. 'Bermuda might be more than you bargained for. There could be much better prospects from every direction if you stayed here. Possibly Robin might persuade you.'

Later Robin, as if taking Guy's advice seriously, attacked her. 'You must be out of your mind!'

'I would be if I accepted such a position.' Celia didn't pretend not to understand him.

Robin replied with what she considered a complete lack of discretion, 'If Guy has taken a fancy to you, then you're made for life. Good heavens, I've never heard of him even trying before. Usually he just lifts his little finger and all the girls come running.'

'How very delicately you put it,' she cried scornfully. 'But it's a business proposition he's interested in, not, I'm sure, some illicit love affair.'

'Well, whatever it is, I can hardly believe you're not interested. You must be, even if only slightly.' Robin regarded her faintly flushed cheeks with a frowning perplexity.

Celia glanced at him, then away again, conscious of the rapid beating of her heart. Robin was asking her to admit to something she would rather not. She was interested, this much she knew, in spite of all her protestations otherwise.

73

Yet it was difficult to know how the idea of working for a man one disliked could be enticing. It was something she would need time to puzzle out. Meanwhile Robin waited, full of curiosity. That much, if nothing else, was plainly obvious!

She said carefully, 'If such a job had been anywhere else but at this store, I might have been tempted, especially as I've found I'm rather homesick for Manchester. But in the present circumstances, no. A thousand times no, my dear brother!'

Yet she didn't feel nearly so emphatic as she made her way home later in the afternoon. Guy had left quite early after lunch, being called away in person by an extremely attractive brunette, who apart from a brief nod in Robin's direction hadn't lingered to be introduced to Celia.

'She's the girl whom Denis Ryland is supposed to be interested in, but he's out this morning,' Robin confided in a stage-whisper, almost before a suddenly smiling Guy had whipped her from the office. 'Myself, I think she's much more interested in Guy.'

'Don't be silly,' Celia had retorted coldly, and for no good reason she could think of she felt glum. 'Have you decided about Christmas yet?' she queried, attempting to get a proper answer. Robin was so difficult to pin down. 'It was you who sent for me,' she continued, 'so you might appear to owe me a little attention now that I'm here. In fact,' she finished severely, 'I'm really beginning to wonder why I'm here at all.'

Robin hadn't appeared to notice her abrupt attempt to steer the conversation away from the Rylands. 'I did have good reason for sending for you,' he said peevishly. Then, more moderately, 'Quite frankly, Celia, I'm terrified of losing my job, and Lucy doesn't seem to care. As I've already told you, her recklessness astounds me, and I'm quite certain neither of us would last five minutes if Guy should find out. And now that you're apparently doing your utmost to displease him, I'm almost convinced my fate is already sealed. Were I to refuse to spend Christmas at Cheverly there wouldn't be any doubt about it. I'm sorry, Celia, but much as I regret it that's exactly how I feel.'

The decision to go to Cheverly herself came before Celia had gone very far. The whole situation—Robin's attitude together with Lucy's—disheartened her, flooding her mind with illogical thoughts she couldn't suppress, motivating her to act as she would not otherwise have done. Seeing Guy Ryland so obviously enthralled with another woman had aroused some stormy impulsiveness within her which she failed to understand.

Instinctively she felt it was something she would live to regret even while she couldn't resist it. It was like the end of an era, the beginning of a new one, and smouldering in between the ashes of her futile struggle to escape any personal involvement. Her face grew remote, enigmatic. Perhaps she had been a fool to hesitate over Cheverly in the first place? A beautiful house, everything provided, no necessity to worry over tedious household chores. As Robin had pointed out, she would be mad to go on refusing. Wasn't she young and far from unattractive, at an age when slaving over a hot stove held little real appeal? If her visit to Manchester was proving to be one vast fiasco, then she could have nothing to lose by ending it in the luxurious comfort of Guy Ryland's home.

Yet such a decision did not come easily, and Celia shrank away from a closer appraisal of her motives, from a detailed scrutiny of the real reasons behind it. As she walked along the street towards the bus stop, having refused Robin's suddenly generous offer of a taxi, she halted on impulse to stare at herself in one of the huge, gleaming shop windows. She saw not her own slender image reflected in the glass, but another, much younger Celia whom it had replaced. The girl who had so often found a warm solace in wandering these very streets when something distressed her. How many times had she gained comfort from the very anonymity they so unwittingly provided?

The hundreds of unknown faces, the hurrying masses of the crowded industrial city, had always seemed to wrap her in a warm cocoon of sympathy. The stretching, rather frightening, grimy size of it that Aunt Mary always hated was her birthplace, steeped in her very blood, tethering her by fine, invisible threads, so strong she could almost physically feel them. Dear old work-weary, powerful Manchester. How did one ever escape it? Suddenly there were tears, dampening Celia's cold cheeks as her expression changed to painful intensity. She turned away blindly from the window. How did one get rid of something bred in one's bones? Simply to live elsewhere achieved nothing. Places could be much worse than people. Cities like Manchester were so willing to let you go, but inexorably they called one back, using men like Guy Ryland unashamedly to gain their own ends! .

Scarcely aware of anything but the chaotic entanglement of her thoughts, Celia walked on along the crowded pavements of Market Street, letting the jumbled upsurge of too-long-suppressed emotions carry her far from her original bus stop. Why did she have to feel any sort of affinity at all? Through its famous textile industries Manchester had become a power to be reckoned with centuries ago, quickly becoming a leading industrial area—indeed of the whole world! But Celia's own great-grandfather had just worked in a mill; he hadn't owned one, as the Rylands had. Therein, she supposed angrily, lay the difference. Her ancestors had been master spinners, never driven by a passion to rule and dominate. A legacy which Guy Ryland had so obviously had passed down to him!

It was his prerogative, some might say, that he had learned early the thrust and parry of the commercial world. Her father had learned too late! Ryland mills had expanded into the retail trade, developing a country-wide chain of shops as an outlet for their own manufactured goods. Ronald Kingsley had merely tried to expand the business of one shop and failed. The only evidence that he had ever existed lay in his name, which for some reason Guy Ryland still retained above the door.

Celia, drifting down the street on sad memories, came to with a start. It was almost dark and too cold to be walking aimlessly around. Swiftly she rubbed her tear-damp cheeks and caught the first convenient bus to Moorland Road. At the nearest supermarket she bought a fresh chicken along with other items necessary to make a good meal; fresh vegetables, a bottle of wine, some freshly ground coffee.

On arriving home, almost before she was through the door, the telephone rang. 'I've been trying to reach you this past hour,' Guy Ryland told her as she picked up the receiver. 'Where have you been?'

'I'm sorry!' Celia drew a deep breath on the count of ten, but while she managed to remain civil, she offered no explanation.

Apparently he wasn't really interested in one, as he didn't wait for an answer. 'I forgot to give you a message from Mrs Timpson,' he continued impatiently, 'and I don't want to upset her. She wonders if you'd try to find a book of her favourite recipes which she left in your kitchen cupboard. She says you'll know which one she means.'

'After all this time?' Celia's pulse slowed to normal.

'She hasn't liked to bother Robin or Lucy.'

'Oh, I see.'

'I'm sorry I had to leave so quickly,' he added.

'But not unwillingly!' It was out before she could hold her tongue, and immediately she regretted the impulsive words, reluctant that he might think she'd noticed even that much.

'Definitely not!' His enthusiasm came clearly over the line, enraging her further. He added, 'I do hope you're considering my proposition?'

'I might be, Mr Ryland.' In view of her decision to accept his hospitality, there seemed nothing else she could say. Swiftly, feeling as she so often did with him an urge

77

to escape, she added, 'Please tell Mrs Timpson I'll look out her book. Goodnight.'

It wasn't night—just late afternoon, and it didn't occur to Celia until after she had rung off to wonder why Timmy hadn't telephoned herself. After all, the matter had been purely domestic.

CHAPTER FIVE

IT might seem irrational, but once having made up her mind about something Celia always felt honour bound to go through with it, even before anyone but herself was aware of her decision. And so she arrived with Robin and Lucy at Cheverly on Christmas Eve.

The only alternative would have been to spend Christmas on her own in an empty house, and while in London this might not have upset her, in Manchester, for some inexplicable reason, she found the prospect strangely frightening. And to return to London at this late hour would only seem foolish, even irresponsible, with family affairs in their present state. As Robin said, if Guy Ryland was prepared to pay, why not let him? By doing so she was probably only living up to the cynical opinion he appeared to have of herself and Lucy, and if he thought of them already as mercenary and selfish the mere act of eating his food and drinking his wine couldn't possibly lower them any more in his estimation!

Cheverly, when they reached it, was wrapped in almost total darkness, but Mrs Timpson, running through from the kitchen quarters, switched on all the lights.

'I can never get used to the fact that I'm no longer bound by strict economy,' she beamed tactlessly, 'but I was busy with dinner and there was no one else here.'

'Mr Ryland's aunt?' It was Celia who asked the question as Timmy led the way upstairs.

'Oh, she hasn't arrived,' Mrs Timpson paused on the second step, glancing backwards over her shoulder. 'She's not well, apparently. Her companion rang only an hour ago. Nothing serious. I believe, but her doctor has advised her to stay in bed.'

Celia, hearing Lucy mumble behind her, 'Thank goodness for that,' attempted, as she remembered doing in childhood, to cover up such a regrettable lapse. 'I'm sorry,' she said, over-loudly, and added at random the first thing to enter her head. 'In view of this, Mr Ryland could have gone abroad after all.'

Her impulsive comment sounded irrational even to her own ears, and she wasn't surprised that Timmy glanced at her questioningly for a few seconds before she obviously remembered. 'Oh well,' Mrs Timpson shrugged philosophically, 'it's a bit too late for that, although I suppose he might have done. Now, if you like, I'll show you your rooms before I get on with the evening meal.'

As they had done years ago, without another word, even from Lucy, they trooped behind her up the wide staircase. Someone would see to their luggage straight away, she promised before she left them at their respective doors.

Celia's bedroom, like the bathroom attached to it, was beautiful, and once again she found herself almost envious of such luxury. Throwing her coat and handbag on to a pink, brocaded chair, she walked swiftly across the floor and sat down experimentally on the edge of the low, satin-covered bed. Her shoes came off with a light flick and she dug her narrow toes into the velvet depth of the carpet with a sensuous sigh, even while she regretted that part of her which revelled in such extravagant surroundings. To live thus could become a habit, something one could too easily become used to. Besides, there was nothing to be gained from sitting here dreaming wild dreams which could never come true.

79

As her luggage arrived Celia jumped to her feet and began to unpack, storing away the few things she had brought in the commodious fitted cupboards which lined one of the walls. These were painted in a smooth, silken white and decorated in gold, so beautifully done that she scarcely dared touch them. In surprise she decided that she must have been put in one of the main guest apartments. Lucy and Robin were on the next floor, where she did remember Timmy saying most of the spare rooms were placed. For no logical reason Celia felt very cut off, a feeling she dismissed instantly as ridiculous. The next floor was only up a short flight of stairs, so she wasn't altogether isolated!

Swiftly she bathed and dressed, not wishing to linger with such confusing thoughts. She wore a long dress in a plain, unadorned black which she imagined gave her poise, and would, she hoped, help her to merge into the background. Timmy had mentioned that Christmas Eve was usually informal, with neighbours coming in for drinks after dinner, a custom instigated by Guy's mother and one which he saw no reason to dispose of.

Her brief toilet complete, Celia decided against going to see if Lucy was ready. In spite of the apparent warmth of Lucy's welcome on that first morning after she arrived the girl seemed to have changed. Try as she might Celia seemed unable to re-establish their old relationship. They didn't even appear to have much in common any more, if, Celia was beginning to wonder, they ever had. Yet Celia could have sworn that Lucy had been genuinely glad to see her, and had received the impression that she couldn't wait to have a heart-to-heart talk.

Could it be, Celia wondered, that it was she herself who had changed, had grown into someone whom Lucy found in some way unapproachable? Perhaps this was the obvious explanation for a reception grown strangely cool. Even when Robin had mentioned Guy's offer of a job at the store, Lucy had been far from enthusiastic, openly agreeing with

Celia about her decision not to accept it. Almost as if she would be pleased to see the last of her!

Everything made for confusion! As the days slipped by this much only had become clear, and no one, not even Timmy, seemed able to help very much. This Christmas, Celia hoped rather desperately as she closed her bedroom door might, if it provided only one clue to this bewildering puzzle, be worth the sacrifice she felt she was making in coming here.

Downstairs, to Celia's dismay, she found Guy Ryland waiting. In the wide hall he stood looking up at her as she came down, his dark eyes glimmering as he appraised her simple black dress.

'We have an hour before dinner,' he informed her as she reached the bottom tread, in a manner which seemed to accuse her of intruding too soon upon his privacy.

'I know,' she replied, with a slight tilt to her chin which from the sudden narrowing of his glance he appeared to find familiar. She hadn't intended to sound defiant, this she considered to be childish, but she had no intention of explaining that she had felt too restless to remain in her room. She wasn't sure whether it was mutual antagonism or a blind chemistry which drew them together. Whatever it was, it was a far from comfortable emotion, one which she strove to escape. Her eyes travelled hopefully in the direction of the kitchen. 'Perhaps I can do something for Mrs Timpson,' she suggested quickly. 'I did remember to look out the cookery book she asked for, but I forgot to give it to her.'

Guy Ryland smiled slightly. 'Mrs Timpson has plenty of help,' he assured her, 'you would only be in the way. If you really want to be useful you can assist me in the decorating of one tree. People will call, and at the moment it looks rather bare.'

'A tree?' Her eyes enormous, Celia stared up at him. She hadn't had a tree for years, and now nostalgically her thoughts veered backwards into the hazy past, when Christmas could never have been complete without one.

His eyes mocked her revealing face. 'Do you find it so daunting, the hanging of a few baubles, or are you silenced by sheer surprise that I should occasionally enjoy something like this?'

Unwittingly, by misconstruing her distress he slanted the limelight from her own vulnerableness, enabling her to retort caustically, 'Tolerate perhaps. But enjoy—no, I'm afraid I can't believe you.'

His voice came hard and deliberate. 'You've never been fond of giving me the benefit of the doubt, so the pattern fits. However, enjoyable or not, the job is to be done and our hour will soon disappear at this rate.'

Relentlessly for another moment his eyes pinned hers, then he turned on his heel, and silenced she followed him to the drawing room. The tree was large, dominating one corner, its wide, spreading branches a frosted blue-green, waiting like a lady to be adorned. At least this was the impression Celia received as she crossed the floor to gaze at it entranced. Not even Guy Ryland's dictatorial presence behind her could distract from the pleasure which flooded her at the sight of such a wonderful tree. She wondered aloud why they didn't have it in the hall.

'Habit, I suppose,' Guy Ryland shrugged. 'My mother liked it here because she was fond of the room and sat here a lot. I would have preferred the hall myself, but never gave it a thought, I'm afraid. I expect Mrs Timpson just told the men to put it up in here as usual.'

Despite the casual flavour of his words, something bleak in his tone deterred Celia from asking more. Thoughtfully she picked up a pile of tinsel and began to thread it lightly over the straight spikes of pine needles. He probably missed his mother a lot more than was obvious, but then a man like Guy Ryland never would wear his heart on his sleeve. He would leave the world to guess the depth of his emotions.

If anyone had told Celia that her reasoning in that moment was almost charitable, she would merely have laughed. Her compassion, she might have retorted, had nothing to do with her personal opinion of Guy Ryland. The more she knew of him the more she disliked the man. That his proximity should affect her more deeply each time she was with him she discounted as sheer imagination.

She draped the last of the tinsel and he suggested mildly, 'You'd better start on these fragile glass balls. You'll cope with them easier than I would with your slender fingers.'

Instinctively, before quite realising what she was doing, Celia flipped her hands behind her back, her pulse jerking. It was uncanny that his light reference to her fingers should seem to stress an intimacy which didn't exist between them. Swiftly, her cheeks flushed and she forced herself to relax, to disregard such foolishness, to pretend to become absorbed with what she was doing. 'Did your mother decorate her tree herself?' she asked, pursuing the very subject she had decided to drop. Her cheeks were still hot and her pulse had not yet steadied completely, and she deplored the state to which he seemed so easily able to reduce her.

'Yes,' Guy replied from the top of the ladder, 'She was only in her sixties and extremely active. There seemed no reason why she shouldn't.'

At loss for something further to add, Celia grasped a luminous coloured ball too quickly and impaled on her thumb a million splinters of glittering glass. 'Ouch!' she exclaimed. It was one of those peculiar incidents which normally cause pain but in this instance did not. Not, at least, during the first few seconds, and Celia's short exclamation was prompted more by fright than anything else.

Unaware of this Guy was off the ladder in a trice. Celia's hand was grasped with a muttered word of impatience. 'What on earth have you done now?'

Celia's cheeks, which had paled with shock, flushed to a rosy red as he held her slender wrist and brushed the clinging fragments from her hand. His clasp touched raw

83

nerves, sending lightning currents upwards right to her sensitive, shaking mouth.

'Stop worrying!' His voice was curt, mistaking the quiver which ran through her body for fear. 'There's very little damage. It's scarcely even bleeding apart from a few tiny pricks.' With a suddenly teasing grin at her taut face he did as she had often done herself as a child. Gently he placed her finger with its tiny speck of blood against his mouth where she could actually feel his lips soothing the small sore abrasion.

Convulsively unable to move, Celia shivered, her breath catching audibly in her throat. 'Please don't,' she whispered, her voice curiously strangled as a hot surge of feeling threatened to overcome her. Momentarily she felt paralysed, helpless in his grasp, unable to move. The movement of his lips against her hand was somehow not to be borne.

Slowly, and somewhat reluctantly it seemed, he released her finger while still holding her arm, his steel-keen glance fastening on her rose-pink mouth. 'Cured,' he quipped mockingly, 'if in a rather unconventional fashion. Don't you approve?'

His eyes told her that he was quite aware she did not, and that he was also aware of the emotion he had so deliberately aroused within her. He enjoyed teasing her and she hated him for it, yet it was difficult to express such feelings with her mind in such a ridiculous chaos. And before she could collect her scattered wits for a reply of some suitability he continued, still with a tormenting gleam in his eye, as if he read her thoughts.

'I can assure you a cure was all I had in mind, but perhaps it would have been better to have done it this way.'

Swiftly he lowered his dark head and the heat in her body exploded to a thunderstorm as his lips touched hers. It was a kiss of supreme briefness, almost experimental, like someone savouring a new recipe to ascertain that the flavour was exactly right.

Not in so many words was Celia to know the outcome of such a brief survey. There was the softness of touch, a moment's hesitation, then like lightning striking his lips hurt and his hands crushed. She struggled only briefly against his cruel grip, but in the subsequent flame and confusion of fire she became aware that he held her away from him again and was explaining to Robin that his sister had given herself a fright when a glass decoration broke.

Fortunately Robin was not especially given to close scrutiny. He was essentially a dreamer, his head too far in the clouds to notice the bottomless chasm at his sister's feet. 'Celia is often too enthusiastic to notice any danger in small things,' he said lightly. Apparently dismissing any possibility of her being really hurt, he turned, instantly diverted by the tree which stood in all its sparkling glory, complete even to the glittering fairy on top. 'I missed ours,' he allowed generously, 'after Celia went. I'm afraid it's a custom we take for granted until suddenly it's not there any more.'

There was a slight pause, an uncomfortable hesitation as, ignoring Robin, Celia's stormy eyes flashed over Guy Ryland's dark, handsome face, the wickedly sardonic mouth. 'If you'll excuse me!' she managed to get out.

'That's the dinner gong,' he drawled, totally unembarrassed, not prepared to notice tantrums or to exaggerate a small incident which had passed. He even had the audacity to take her arm, ostensibly, she supposed, to give the impression of polite solicitude, which didn't impress her one bit.

Fretfully she jerked away from him, her flushed cheeks paling, unable to bear his touch again no matter what his present intentions. It was too much like the scrape of raw metal against steel, the ensuing sparks scorching and burning. Yet while she longed to devastate him equally with an annihilating glare, her glance as she stalked past him reached no further than the faint smile which edged his frankly cynical lips.

85

Why should he indulge in such behaviour? The question hammered through Celia's head for the remainder of the evening. All through dinner—all through the hours which followed, when what appeared to be literally crowds of people called for drinks and coffee and hot mince pies. These latter, supplied in huge quantities by an indefatigable Mrs Timpson, proved extremely popular, and there were all kinds of other small delicacies which she could see were greatly appreciated even by some of the more sophisticated, but there was very little she seemed able to eat herself.

If the circumstances had been different, Celia told herself, the evening would have been enjoyable. There was no one there that she had known personally before, but those who knew Lucy and Robin accepted her without question, if not without interest. Celia's smooth, glowing beauty was not the sort to be overlooked anywhere, and the fact that she was here as a guest and that Guy Ryland seemed never far from her side gave rise to a not unnatural speculation.

'I don't have any designs on your family silver!' she muttered in a fierce little aside when, in one instance, his other guests faded away as he stood near her. She hadn't imagined how difficult it could be to be rude to a man in his own house, especially as she had apparently accepted his hospitality, but her nerves were too tense to prevent a protest of some sort.

'A pity, perhaps,' he drawled obliquely, slanting her a studied glance. Then, innocently, 'My vigilance is in no way prompted by suspicion regarding your movements.'

'Yet not from a fond regard, surely?' It wasn't meant to be a question, yet it sounded like one, and she would have given anything to have been able to take it back.

He shrugged, his heavy brows lifting, his eyes exploring her exquisite face. 'I'm still trying to work it out for myself. Right now you're the most decorative thing in the room. I have a great fancy to have you painted in oils and hung in

86

my library. I have known myself to become quite enamoured by a beautiful painting.'

She was incensed, but as much by her thudding heart as his remark, made with such indifferent coolness. 'I should dislike being regarded merely as an *objet d'art,* although even through my own eyes I can't see myself as that.'

'Oh, come, Celia,' he moved a fraction nearer, his eyes mocking her apparent naïveté. 'A London model should surely have learnt to take such compliments in her stride. I considered you would know all the moves.'

Something in his voice, an indefinable meaning to his words, stung her to fury. 'I'm not sure what you imply, but whatever it is I'm aware it's not very pleasant. And I by no means qualify as a model, from London or anywhere else. I've only done shows for the store.'

'And TV.'

'Twice.'

'And Bermuda?' His tone was laced with more than a hint of derision.

Her voice stiffened with resentment. 'I hadn't quite decided.'

'Ah—but you said . . . !' his mouth twisted sarcastically.

'I said I was going to London. I might change my mind about anything else,' she put in hastily.

'So—why not Bermuda? Why the hesitation?'

'I don't have to explain! It's not your business,' her voice came taut with a determined resistance. She was in the middle course of a fast running river. On one side the conventionally safe world she had grown used to, on the other, the wholly diabolical pull of this man's personality, threatening to submerge her in a veritable whirlpool which would destroy her in its dark drowning depth. 'You can't make me explain,' she reiterated again parrot-wise because her breath came strangely.

His mocking laughter came low, and they might have been completely isolated instead of among a crowd of people. 'No, Celia, you don't have to dot your i's or cross your very shaky t's with me. You're hovering on the brink, not having the necessary courage to take that wholly committing step forward. Why?'

'Why?' This time a little of the fight went out of her as her eyes raised helplessly to his face. She wasn't altogether conscious of her surrender. 'Don't you see? I'm twenty-three. In another few years I could easily be too old. I'm trying to take a longer view of my future.'

'That could be sensible,' he said, his eyes curiously watchful, qualifying the slight approval in his tone, 'if you're doing just that. Or is there pressure?'

'Pressure?' the word rebounded from her lips with a returning antagonism, her eyes widening on his rather wildly. Why should he think that? Her thoughts spun erratically. There was Joe—if that was what he meant. With Joe she wasn't sure why she was on the defensive, but she wouldn't allow Guy Ryland to guess. Why should she read more into Joe's eagerness for her to join him than was on the surface? Was it simply her own normal reaction to men, the reluctance to get too personally involved? With Joe there was only a definite desire not get too mixed up with him. With Guy Ryland every bit of her, every sensitive nerve end, screamed out against any further contact, because for some reason she couldn't fathom each time he touched her there was a searing current that threatened to throw her completely out of control. It was a crazily unpredictable hotchpotch of emotions with hate, she supposed, as the motivating factor.

Hazily she became aware that Guy, impatient of her prolonged silence, was almost spelling it out for her. He muttered tersely, 'Is someone urging you against your will?'

'I do know what you mean,' she retorted, defensively pulling herself together, 'but once again I might remind you it's none of your business.'

'It must be,' he reasoned, 'if I want you to work for me.'

Why was he always too quick for her, with his well-

88

trained brain usually one step ahead? He had an answer to everything, never floundering in the depth of confusion as she did only too often. The knowledge annoyed, so that she used recklessly the first reprisal to enter her head. 'I don't want to work for you, though,' she uttered breathlessly, knowing she was too impulsive, yet unable to find anything else to say.

'You've quite decided?'

She sensed the underlying malice in his question, and wondered with some perplexity why her staying should be in any way important to him. And, because it seemed easier to defy him than to waver on even one point, she found herself nodding emphatically.

'Which doesn't answer my question!' Impatiently he dismissed her nod that told him only the half of what he wished to know.

Stubbornly she threw discretion to the wind. 'But my decision, Mr Ryland, could in no way affect you personally.'

'That,' he replied enigmatically, 'could depend on many things. The store does need you, and, as I am the store, you must judge for yourself. The important thing at the moment is to make sure you change your mind, and in this the personal approach is often the only way when all else fails.'

With what she hoped was a cool smile Celia moved away from him and attached herself to a group engaged in the earnest discussion of trivial things, and was relieved when, apparently guessing that the conversation would be of no particular interest, he made no attempt to follow. Nor did he accompany the small group with whom she went to Midnight Service in the village church, but he was waiting when they returned and there was more hot coffee and sandwiches, and the air seemed full of people wishing each other a Merry Christmas. It was only after the last of his guests had departed that Guy, murmuring a brief goodnight, disappeared in the direction of his study.

'Quite probably he'll be there for several hours,' Mrs Timpson, who had gone with the party to church, told Celia as she helped to carry the last of the used cups to the kitchen. Lucy and Robin, who showed no eagerness to help, had retired to their rooms. 'I do wish Mr Ryland would try to relax more,' Mrs Timpson added, putting down her laden tray with a sigh.

Celia shrugged, making no reply, as Timmy switched off the kitchen lights and closed the door. If Guy chose to work through all the hours of the night, far be it for her to make any comment, but surely there must be something wrong with a man who put work before everything, even Christmas!

For Celia it was a bad night. She found it almost impossible to sleep, remembering everything that had taken place, particularly the incident in the drawing-room beside the tree. Her bed was as it had looked, supremely comfortable, but in the early hours she switched on her table lamp and tried to read a magazine. It was no good—the pages and print danced before her tired eyes and, feeling quite weary and disconsolate, she stared around her beautiful room, aware more of the taut state of her nerves than the indisputable luxury of her surroundings.

She wasn't sure of the time when she heard Guy Ryland walk upstairs, but she was conscious of her quickening heartbeats. Somehow she hadn't imagined his footsteps in the corridor outside could endue such a sense of intimacy. There was worse to come when she suddenly realised he was next door, his unhurried movements through the thickness of the wall faint but unmistakable. Once again she had the feelings of a small fish caught in a net which was being deliberately, if indirectly, tightened. He might consider her naïve—his own word—but a man like Guy Ryland would be way beyond the experience of the average girl, and she would be very much wiser, she knew it instinctively, to pack straight away and return to London. Nothing since she had returned to Manchester had gone as she had planned, and there was no reason to believe that at this late hour it would begin to do so!

She got up early and ran down to the hall. It was barely half-past eight, but she found it impossible to stay in bed any longer, because her uneasy slumbers were too disturbed by impossible dreaming. She saw through the window that snow was falling again, but only lightly. Even so, Celia loved it. It seemed to emphasise the loneliness of the landscape. To give a sense of isolation to a house which she realised wasn't actually isolated at all, but the ensuing whiteness as the snow fell made it appear solitary, beautiful, remote. There was no wind, but this would come, stinging with frost from the snow-capped mountains of the Lakes, bringing an evening which might be cold as death, but would ensure fires piled high with logs and the bitter, all prevailing scent of wood-smoke.

There was no one in the breakfast room when she found it, although the table was laid ready and a pot of hot coffee stood half empty on the snowy cloth with one used cup beside it. It was still warm and Celia helped herself, wondering idly who had been here before her. It might have been Guy Ryland, most probably it had been a man, but whoever it was had left no obvious clues as to his identity.

Suddenly the quietness made her feel restless. Nothing or no one appeared to be stirring and she felt reluctant to disturb Mrs Timpson with her army of helpers in the kitchen. Her experience of Timmy of old on Christmas morning did nothing to encourage her in this direction.

Swiftly she went back to her room and found a warm, hooded coat and swung it carelessly around her shoulders. The coat was a pale, tawny shade that almost exactly matched her hair, and her thin wool blouse beneath it in a cool clear blue which echoed the translucent colour of her eyes. She ran out through the front door, her hair on this rare occasion unrestricted, flying behind her, the strands thick and gleaming, seeming almost to have a life of their own.

She walked quickly away from the house towards some not so distant woods. Among the trees it would be quiet and she wanted time to think. She walked across the level field towards it, gazing around her as she went. From here no other house was visible. A few muted, faraway sounds drifted up, but within the confines of the dark wood all was silent.

Over the low stone wall that split the wood from the field she went, her feet crunching the frosted snow. Then, to her surprise, she found Guy Ryland walking just ahead of her. Dismay held her momentarily still as her pleasure in the morning faded. It had been he who had had the coffee, and he must have left the house before her. She had imagined him still in bed. Perhaps he was one of these supermen who could do without sleep!

Prepared to overlook her own restless state, Celia stared at his retreating figure apprehensively. He was the last person she wished to encounter, especially this morning, but she could scarcely accuse him of trespassing on his own land. Cautiously she lifted her foot to turn, but carelessly her toe caught the end of a brittle branch, and the sharp snap of it echoed loudly, or so it seemed, through the static morning air.

Naturally he heard, and swinging round abruptly he turned and saw her. 'Good morning, Celia,' he called solemnly, retracing his steps, coming up to her. 'I hope you slept well?'

'Thank you,' she said stiffly, well aware that from her shadowed eyes he could see she had not. Flakes of snow drifted through an open space in the trees, falling silvery white on her cheek. With suddenly nervous fingers she brushed them off. 'I didn't intend going far,' she murmured blankly, letting her eyes rest for one brief moment on the cleft of his strong chin. 'I think I'll go back now.'

His eyes narrowed intently on the wild rose colour of

her face, the agitated tremor at the corner of her betraying mouth. The glint in his eyes deepened as he put up his hand to brush the protective hood from her hair. Over her shoulders the fluffy thickness of it tumbled brightly. 'I like your hair,' he said slowly. 'You should never cover it up.'

Her heart was beating, sharp, uneven thuds that hurt even as she jerked away from his touch. In attempted defiance she tried to put back her hood, but his fingers caught hers, staying the act. 'When will you learn to stop fighting me?' he exclaimed roughly, as if such a thing was important.

She turned her head towards the shape of him which grew insubstantial and indistinct as rage blurred her eyesight, but she was too wise to answer his challenge directly. 'Why do you choose to make an issue over small things? The state of my hair can't possibly matter to you!'

He was as accomplished in the art of evasion as she was. 'I merely suggested you tried to relax. You might find it less wearing than fighting me.'

'I'm not sure . . .' Her legs felt weak, maybe from walking in the snow, and her brow felt clammy from apparent exhaustion. She glanced up at him, her lips parted as she sought to convey a more adamant refusal, only to find her vision blocked as he bent his dark head and his lips came down on her half open ones.

Shocked by what seemed to be becoming a ridiculous habit, she tried to draw away, but once more her traitorous senses defied her. There was nothing like force in his mouth as it moved again in what seemed an experimental manner on hers, and while his hands slid beneath her coat to caress her trembling body, he made no attempt to hold her. But it was as if lightning leapt, holding them irrevocably together. The pressure of his mouth increased only slightly, yet her own clung to his and she clutched him to steady herself. His hands were sure and warm and she was lost in the force of her own response. She could feel his breath coming warmly, blending with hers, stirring in her a flood of longing such as she had never known before.

This time, unlike the last, she knew complete desolation when he let her go. When his hands fell away she wanted only to cling. To the clouded recess of her mind came the pain of bleak denial. Guy made no pretence of being other than in complete control of a situation he might easily have planned, with danger he was quite aware of. His fingers fastened on her racing pulse, his eyes surveyed the trembling unsteadiness of her mouth with ironic satisfaction.

'That,' he mused lightly, disregarding her helpless distraction, 'will do for a start. It must certainly help to get rid of some of your inhibitions. Perhaps it might even assist you in making up your mind to work for me.'

'Never!' How she hated his complacency, and free of him, she felt nothing but contempt for herself. In behaving like a common slut could she ever look at herself in the glass again! Her body cringed where he had touched her and she hated herself more than she hated him. 'If you're merely trying to amuse yourself I suggest you find another candidate. Many girls with much more experience than myself would probably leap at the job.' And you, her eyes added, daring him to contradict her.

He laughed—and coolly at that. 'I fear you underestimate yourself, Celia.'

'Surely I should know myself better than anyone else, Mr Ryland?'

'Mr Ryland!' his firm mouth twisted wryly. 'Do you still find it possible to call me that?'

She flushed, the colour wild beneath her pale skin. 'It comes naturally,' she said, unrelenting.

'So, in your case, would other things,' he taunted, 'if you tried to relax. There are far more enjoyable ways of passing the time than building brick walls around oneself.'

'A girl might need one six feet high with you around,' she flashed back, refusing to be intimidated in this manner,

94

and wishing him to know that her wits could be almost as quick as his on occasion.

He smiled, his glance moving derisively over her wind-swept hair to meet the stormy blue of her indignant eyes. 'You can't pretend that you found my storming of the Bastille entirely repulsive, but if it pleases you I'll try to keep our relationship on a strictly platonic level. I only make one stipulation—that you don't try to tempt me.'

In a fine whirl of fury Celia turned away from his mocking face, her feet slithering drunkenly on the wet snow. How dared he even suggest such a thing! He was in-furiating, deliberately so, she suspected. Suddenly, in spite of the heat of her temper she felt chilled, yet no twinge of gratitude touched her heart as on noticing her slight shiver, Guy proposed mildly,

'Why not come back to the house? I'd be willing to swear you've had no breakfast, and we could walk further after lunch. The snow might have cleared by then.'

This time she made no protest, not even when he took her arm and led her back by a shorter path than that by which she had come. Perhaps he was right, her stomach did feel strangely empty, although breakfast was a meal she rarely bothered with as a rule, but the peculiar feeling per-sisted and she could only put it down to hunger. 'There was no one about,' she explained, 'when I left. I didn't feel like eating alone.'

'You won't this morning,' Guy Ryland promised. 'Christ-mas is a morning when no one should ever be alone.'

Celia glanced at him, slanting him a swiftly inquiring stare from under long lashes. He sounded almost human, or was it that their conversation suddenly attained heights of formality that didn't ring true? But there was nothing in his hard, dark face to indicate one way or another that this was so, and she looked away from him again, over the white snow-covered fields as they emerged from the wood.

'Thousands are,' she replied politely, but nonetheless feelingly, into the silence which pressed down on them. If he would, then she would gladly co-operate on this more impersonal basis.

There was a break in the cloud and the snow fell lighter as they walked over the field, and from the direction of Cheverly came a series of loud halloas. Celia could make out two figures waving wildly from the immediate precincts of the house. Surely, she almost stopped in astonishment, not Lucy and Robin? It wasn't yet ten o'clock. She doubted if either had left their beds.

'That will be, I think, my—er—cousin and his friend,' Guy supplied smoothly, before she could ask. 'They did say they would be here early. You did meet Miss Morrison at the store, didn't you, although you weren't introduced.'

Slowly, unconsciously frowning a little, Celia nodded, wondering why she should suddenly feel so cold. It wasn't the inclement weather—the brisk trot she had been doing in order to keep up with Guy's longer strides precluded this. She did remember Greta Morrison only too clearly, yet suddenly she had no longer any interest in meeting her. But as if guessing this with his diabolically astute mind, Guy grasped her arm again and thrust her forward.

CHAPTER SIX

THAT Christmas which she spent at Cheverly was one which Celia never entirely forgot; small incidents returned to haunt her long after they ought to have faded from her memory. The loveliness of the house and snow-covered grounds might have receded from her thoughts in time, but always with her during the ensuing days after she left there was the lingering closeness of Guy Ryland in the wintry woods, and in the drawing room, by the tree.

On Christmas morning she had been duly introduced

to his new visitors, but hadn't found the experience very enlightening. Denis Ryland, slimly built and of medium height, was nothing like Guy to look at, and had seemed an extremely self-opinionated young man, and Greta Morrison just as self-assured a young woman. After the first five minutes Celia decided that Robin had been right in his remarks that Greta had a definite fondness for Guy. However, she summarised dryly, having watched the girl flirting with both, she looked as if she would settle for either of them, given the chance!

Half ashamed of what she had condemned in herself as uncharitable thoughts, Celia had contrived to look the other way, but the turning of that blind eye hadn't been easy. Guy, saddled with a houseful of gay young people, had seemed by no means reluctant in his duties as a host. Clearly he found the lovely Greta attractive, and while he might have her earmarked for Denis, wasn't above a little light dalliance himself.

Where Lucy came in all this Celia couldn't be sure. She had noticed her exchanging several swift glances with Denis, and once a slight touching of hands when apparently they thought no one was looking, but apart from this there had been nothing even remotely indiscreet which might have betrayed them to a casual onlooker.

Yet despite Celia's uneasiness the days of Christmas passed with surprising swiftness, and after Boxing Day, when it was time to go home, she felt a curious reluctance to leave Cheverly. There was inside her traitorous heart a vague longing which she refused to define.

Two days after the New Year she rang the store and asked if she could see Guy Ryland.

'I doubt it, Miss Kingsley,' his secretary said, 'he is extremely busy and has appointments for the whole afternoon. He specifically told me he wasn't available to anyone.'

'Would you please confirm this?' Celia persisted, while wondering why. She had no reason to believe he would cancel such an order for the sake of a girl who had opposed him on every overture he had ever made to improve their relationship.

Seconds later his secretary spoke again, obviously flustered. 'Mr Ryland will see you right away,' she said, 'or any time you like.'

Unhappily Celia couldn't decide what to wear. What did one wear to inform a man like Guy Ryland of a change of mind? Her decision hadn't been easy, and this was only, she realised, the first step. She didn't imagine he would be in any way prepared to smooth the way for her. During Christmas at Cheverly she had quarrelled persistently with him until he had looked quite murderous at times. Any attempt by her now to ask for concessions was probably doomed to failure.

To help boost her wavering courage she put on her most stylish skirt, topping it with a thin sweater which clung neatly to the slender curves of her figure. She was aware she would need all the confidence she could muster and more, and that her appearance was the only thing she could hope to count on. Too often her tongue was too impulsive and her nerves too taut.

Despair ran frighteningly through her as she arranged her long hair and carefully applied fresh make-up. Guy Ryland would never understand how difficult it had been. Even now she wasn't quite sure exactly what was behind her own change of mind. She wanted to believe it was solely because of Lucy, that the glimpse she had had of the girl's distraught face when caught unawares had been wholly responsible, but at the bottom of her heart she knew that this was not so, not altogether. In the end she put it down to an all-prevailing fondness for her home town and her renewed desire to spend at least some of her working life there.

Before going to the store she contacted her employer in London, her father's old friend, and told him what she intended to do. The more personal details she left out, but she did try to explain a little about her recent family problems as, although they didn't share a very deep friendship, Philip Newman had been kind and she felt in many ways indebted to him. Besides, she felt sure Guy Ryland would inquire if she had left this particular escape hatch open, and there might be some measure of satisfaction to be gained from telling him she had not.

Next she got in touch with Aunt Mary, who didn't appear to mind or to be even surprised, for that matter.

'I'll stay in Torquay for the rest of the winter,' she said brightly, adding lightly, 'I think you're doing the right thing.'

If only she could be as sure as Mary, Celia fretted as she started out. In retrospect it seemed that she had been sure of nothing since that day three years ago when the store had been sold, but there was one thing she did feel emphatic about. If Guy Ryland was to hold the taking of this job over her head as a sort of perverted revenge for the slap she'd once given him, then he would be the first to regret it!

She drew a deep breath before entering his office. It was like taking a blind step over a precipice as she felt the jolt of peculiar shock jerk her heart to her throat. Then after the first split second she tried to pull herself together, aware of the frank curiosity in his secretary's eyes as she stood aside for Celia to enter.

Robin was nowhere about. Guy occupied a wing at the other side of the building which appeared to have been newly renovated from what, so far as she could remember, had been an old store room. Now, divided into a spacious suite of offices with modern fitments, she was amazed by the difference. But she also noticed that this was undoubtedly the executive patch from which the main business of the store would be directed. It seemed that Robin no longer sat in the most important position as she had thought.

It could have been this knowledge, too newly realised to allow for dissection, which threw her into a near-panic as the other woman withdrew, closing the door carefully behind her. Wildly Celia stared around, all too clearly searching for a means of escape, and, as if reading her tremulous thoughts, in a flash Guy Ryland was on his feet.

'Do come in, Celia,' he invited blandly, coming around his desk, pulling forward a chair, glancing at it pointedly. 'You'd better sit down. It doesn't become you to stand about dithering. I find it extremely satisfying that you've arrived, but if you had any doubts about it then you should have examined them sooner.'

Beast! It was the first word to enter her mind, although just in time she refrained from saying it aloud, and she lowered her dark lashes as she sat hastily on the proffered chair in case her eyes said it for her. 'I never dither, Mr Ryland,' she retorted coldly, knowing well what he referred to. He would find she could cling quite as tenaciously to an agreement as he could, and once her mind was made up she would not shirk the consequences.

He smiled, a slight smile that scarcely moved his lips. 'I've yet to meet the woman who didn't,' he mocked softly.

'Yet when choosing a candidate for the job you had in mind you surely wouldn't consider one in that category?' she said sharply, forgetting completely her resolve to guard her tongue, infuriated as she was by his self-possession which she envied.

'But you surely haven't come to talk of anything so mundane as work?' he quipped caustically.

'What else?' Deliberately she tried to keep her voice taut as once again, in spite of herself, she remembered how the same lips which were taunting her now had intoxicated her once. She also recaptured the whirlwind of unknown sensations, whose memory had left a deep yearning within her.

'Well—then what can I do for you?' he asked suavely, returning unhurriedly to his own chair.

So he was going to make her spell it out? He didn't intend that her path should be easy. He would find pleasure

100

in seeing her grovel! Tightly Celia's fingers curled around the leather strap of her shoulder bag.

'Robin isn't here?' she inquired somewhat jerkily, seeking to assure herself that at least her brother wouldn't witness her humiliation.

'He is not.' Guy's voice hardened before the anxiousness in hers, and she suddenly remembered his threats.

Defensively her chin came up. 'You made no secret of it, Mr Ryland. I hadn't forgotten. If I don't agree to work for you my brother's position might be at stake.'

'Quite so,' he agreed smoothly, his eyes unrelenting as he watched her angry colour flare. 'I see nothing wrong with a little bartering. Surely the commercial trade began in this fashion and managed nicely without hard cash.'

Celia's hand crept shaking to her throat at the thought of it. 'You might try to be uncivilised,' she choked, 'but you can't bring back outdated customs. In modern terms one could call it blackmail!'

'A little of which is not necessarily harmful,' he demurred, 'if used with the well-being of the victim in mind.'

'However you choose to describe the grabbing of a man's house and almost everything he possesses, I can hardly believe it could be couched pleasantly. Now it seems that the last of your atrocities is to include me!'

His strong head went back at this and he laughed, as if her vibrant little speech merely served to amuse him. 'You wouldn't expect me to leave you out, but how very gently you express yourself, my dear. It could perhaps be my duty to teach you better manners—if you come to me.'

She heeded only the half of what he was saying, but her blood throbbed as she cried hotly, 'I'm scarcely in any position to argue.'

'Whatever you refer to,' Guy drawled enigmatically. 'But to return to the house. I thought I'd already made it clear that the house is yours for as long as you wish.'

'Not your exact words.'

'Just so long as it pleases me, then.'

101

'Exactly! And to please you, Mr Ryland, I have to dance to your tune ...'

'Which would be a charming sight as well as an extremely surprising one.' Again his mouth quirked sarcastically at the corners. 'Perhaps with this in view we might get down to business and keep the lighter side for more appropriate moments. I thought you were no longer interested in coming to work for me?'

Rather fervently Celia wished she wasn't. Even to contemplate such a thing was like plunging head-first into a river of deep water. If she didn't drown on first impact, wasn't it inevitable she would be swept away by the current? 'I find,' she said, all of a rush, 'the thought of coming back to the store appealing.'

'What about Bermuda?' His eyes remained fixed on her face. 'I wouldn't want you to have second thoughts, Miss Kingsley. In fact once you started with me, I couldn't allow them.'

Did he threaten? He had the nerve for it! Yet, as she glanced perceptively at that hard, inflexible mouth, a fleeting premonition made her shiver. How could they ever work amicably together when conflict hovered so tautly between them? 'I rang London,' she heard herself explaining through the confusion in her head, 'I spoke to Philip Newman himself. Everything is cancelled.'

'And if I refused to employ you, or did you count on it?'

'Almost, Mr Ryland,' she exclaimed. 'You certainly left me with no illusions as to what would happen if I did not. But it's only'—she strove to believe she was speaking the truth—'for Robin's sake I'm here. I can assure you that if you've had a change of heart I shall be more than willing to seek employment elsewhere.'

There were undercurrents of mockery in the depth of his eyes. 'Tut, tut, my dear girl. As if I should let such talent as yours escape me! Even your eloquence has a certain appeal. I'm sure it could be put to good use.'

'When can I start?' She was willing her limbs not to tremble.

He looked at her through half-closed lids, as though, surprisingly his mind was not completely on such trivial detail. 'I suggest you start on Monday,' he said, after a minute. 'In the meantime I'll arrange for an office to be put at your disposal, one on this floor. You might conceivably need an assistant, but to begin with I think you must collaborate with me. It would be wiser. I should need to assure myself that we're both working in the same direction.'

Even less happily than before Celia nodded. The thought of working with him personally hadn't occurred to her, and she cared little for the way such an arrangement sent small waves of apprehension coursing through her, quickening the unsteady beat of her heart. 'I wouldn't want to be a nuisance,' she said, shooting him a look of inquiry. 'I believed you only came here on odd occasions.'

'I have in the past but, busy or not, I can always keep an eye on you. As I've already told you, there's too much to be done for me to be absent much longer. You are merely going to help me put this store on its feet, and I think we both enjoy a challenge.'

Celia swallowed, a visible movement in the lovely curve of her throat, and the man's eyes fastened on it speculatively. 'And Robin . . . ?' she uttered.

'Just so long as you co-operate, my girl,' he retorted significantly, suddenly like a man stung to a hard recklessness, 'your brother will have no cause for complaint.'

That evening Lucy attacked her for staying on. 'You must be crazy,' she cried, 'you'll never settle after London.'

'Of course I shall,' Celia declared stoically, realising her dilemma for the first time. She couldn't possibly confess to Lucy her real reason for staying, and looked helplessly at Robin.

For once Robin's wits seemed reasonably sharp. 'I think we'll enjoy Celia's company for a while,' he told his younger sister. Like Celia he felt unable to discuss openly what he

103

knew concerned Lucy as much as any of them, but the thought of having Celia to help cope with Lucy's highly controversial romance brought nothing but relief. If the flame should burst into a furnace, then at least he shouldn't have to contend with Guy Ryland alone! 'Guy seems determined to have her, anyway,' he grinned, trying to introduce a lighter note, but not sure if he had succeeded when Lucy retorted waspishly,

'As long as she doesn't allow his attentions to go to her head! Greta Morrison is the only girl whom he seems at all interested in at the moment. I actually saw her in his arms at Cheverly, at Christmas.'

Celia gulped, feeling the first hard thrust of pain. Desperately she shied away from such a picture, refusing to hold it responsible as she attempted to make her peace with a resentful Lucy. 'Personalities don't come into it,' she managed quietly. 'I'm simply to do a job for which Guy Ryland appears to think I'm well suited. If . . .' she hesitated, but only imperceptibly, 'if I'm to be allowed an assistant, would you care for the position?'

'Me!' Lucy exclaimed coldly. 'No, thank you! I'm doing quite nicely in Accounts. Denis Ryland was saying only the other day, that I definitely have quite a head for figures.'

'So has he!' Robin remarked enigmatically, seeming far from impressed by such a remark as he shared with Celia a glance of some apprehension.

Later both he and Lucy went out, but Timmy rang. 'Mr Ryland has just been telling me the good news,' she said. 'I can't tell you how pleased I am!'

Her words removed a little of the soreness from Celia's heart. At last someone was happy about her staying! 'Thank you, Timmy,' she said.

Prepared to chat as she was, her thread of comfort was rudely snapped when Mrs Timpson went on quickly, 'Miss Morrison is coming to dinner this evening, dear, so I must go. Mr Ryland wanted something special.'

It was not the first time Celia had discovered that hard

work was perhaps the best antidote for a restless mind, and during the next few weeks she almost surprised herself by the amount of work she got through. But if the outcome of hours of sheer industry gradually brought the desired changes to the store, the satisfaction of being one of the team to bring this about was in no way reflected in the paleness of her face. She lost weight, and although this was partly concealed by the animation of her manner, it was obvious to the more discerning onlooker that something disturbed her.

In repose there clung to her soft mouth a sensitive disenchantment, and the faintest aura of suffering clouded the depth of her vivid blue eyes. Deep down she was only half conscious of the cause, only half aware of her own disillusionment as she sought unconsciously to restore to its former untouched state that unawakened part of herself which Guy Ryland had violated in one brief embrace. Work was the one thing which seemed to help when the state of her taunting emotions cried out for release, and it was to this that she turned more and more.

'I didn't ask you to kill yourself,' Guy Ryland said dryly, entering her office late one afternoon. 'You don't have to do it all in one day. Leave a little for later on.'

Celia glanced up, not really startled to find him there. When he was in the store she saw quite a lot of him. He was in and out of her office quite often, but she never got used to having him casually around. He strode in in his abrupt fashion, but while he might convey arrogance this didn't detract from the hard intelligence of his face; the brilliant awareness in his dark eyes that made her heart lunge and antagonism to race in her blood.

Forcing a jagged breath to evenness, she cried impulsively, 'I can't seem to get this plan right for the new showroom on the top floor. Mrs Jenner from the larger ladies' department says none of her ladies would consider trailing all the way up there. She's adamant that we put her on the first floor and leave the younger and more agile to climb to the top.'

'Mrs Jenner appears to have a rare turn of wit.' Guy lowered himself down on to the corner of Celia's desk, swivelling the plan she was studying around to face him. 'We do have escalators and lifts, or does she choose to ignore them?'

'She contends that she has customers who find them uncommonly uncomfortable to manage.'

'While I contend that the vast majority of middle-aged, generously proportioned ladies are often more agile than their slimmer contemporaries, and would more than gladly sacrifice the convenience of the first floor for the additional privacy of the fourth.'

Almost Celia smiled. 'Might I quote you to Miss Jenner, sir, and assure her that you're some authority on the matter?'

'No, you may not!' His lips firmed lightly. 'I only believe in sticking my neck out so far. But it might easily go through the proper channels. It can only amount to what has already been suggested. We can have no shortage of qualified staff working on this project.'

'We have so many,' Celia sighed, a little fretfully, 'what seems to be a veritable army of architects and their followers. Sometimes I feel more than superfluous.'

'I can assure you they don't appear to think so.' Consideringly he stared down at her toil-flushed cheeks. Her hair, usually so immaculate, tumbled untidily over her shoulders, proof, if it was needed, of hours of strenuous activity. She wore only a pair of serviceable jeans together with a rather tightly fitting top, an outfit hastily chosen from a pile of unsold sale articles when some unforseen problems had sprung up. 'That outfit,' he mused, 'seems to represent some sort of invitation. I'd not be willing to hazard a guess.'

Colour flooded wildly beneath her skin at his words, which contained more than a hint of mockery. 'Mr Ryland,' she exploded, regretting, if not for orthodox reasons, her more conventional apparel, 'one can't climb over piles of building materials dressed any other way! And if this was all you came to tell me——' Uncertainly her voice faded as, too late, she remembered he was after all her boss, and she disliked above all things to sound impertinent. 'I mean,' she floundered hastily, 'I can't imagine you came merely to lecture me about this?'

Dark amusement sprang into his eyes, along with a hint of censure. 'I did have it in mind, having caught a glimpse of you about an hour ago—or rather having had my attention drawn by what in my companion almost amounted to a wolf-whistle. But that wasn't all.'

'No?' Swiftly she glanced up, away from the baffling plans which suddenly seemed to be dancing before her tired eyes. Her long, slim fingers, as they brushed the heavy hair from off her hot forehead, felt curiously numb. There was no apprehension in her now, just an overall tiredness.

'I think,' he said, narrowly appraising the bruised shadows beneath her eyes, 'it might be a good idea if you came home with me this evening. I've been going to suggest it for a while. Why burn the midnight oil here when we can do it in comfort at Cheverly? Besides, Mrs Timpson has been begging you to visit her ever since Christmas, you know that.'

The unexpectedness of the invitation shook her somewhat. Even on an entirely business footing it was no light thing to be asked to spend the night at Cheverly. Many angled outrageously for such an invitation and never received one. Yet Celia's nerves reacted strangely and she looked away from him to where the rain ran in silvery rivulets down the uncurtained office window, the darkness of the late January night emphasised by the bright light within. She wasn't quite sure how important he considered the present alterations to the shop, but he did seem keen to have them finished. But apart from this she couldn't ignore a certain eagerness within herself to grasp such an

107

opportunity. It might not come again very quickly, and it would provide a hitherto unavailable chance to speak to him about Denis and Lucy. It was high time, she considered, that this was brought out into the open. Celia knew Lucy and Denis were still seeing each other frequently, but Lucy still chose to wrap their friendship in a clam-like and mysterious silence which continued to worry Robin particularly. Celia didn't forget Guy Ryland's disparaging remarks about her sister at Christmas, nor had she forgiven them, but Lucy had been working hard lately and it was just possible that Guy was in a different frame of mind about her.

Guy broke the strange silence with an irony which brought her up sharply. 'When you've decided the pros and cons of the situation you might be good enough to oblige me with an answer. It's already approaching six o'clock and it's an hour's journey to Cheverly.'

Which was logical, in spite of the thinly veiled sarcasm. Yet, perhaps because she felt so desperately drawn to accepting, she hedged, bearing down firmly on the totally reckless impulses within her. 'If it's about the shop, then I'm sure it could wait until tomorrow. Aren't you always telling me I'm in too much of a hurry? I agree that Timmy's been ringing me, but I can't imagine she'll be looking for me this evening.'

'There are several small details we might well discuss, and you know it.' He ignored Mrs Timpson. 'And while you're there you can stay the night. I'll run you straight back here in the morning. And because you might easily be still sitting here dithering at midnight, I'm making it an order, Miss Kingsley.'

'Yes, Mr Ryland.' Her breath caught and quivered and to hide it she started haphazardly to sweep things from the top of her desk into the relevant drawers, grateful, in some inexplicable way, to have such a decision taken from her. To sleep at Cheverly was something she hadn't contemplated!

'Leave that, for God's sake!' he exclaimed, blunt with impatience as he came to his feet. 'You'll need to pick up a case, I expect. You can always change at Cheverly.'

Quite clearly this implied that he didn't intend she should dine in what she was wearing, and in a moment of rebellion, Celia almost refused. Instead she found herself agreeing, if with a somewhat mutinous expression, 'Of course, Mr Ryland.'

He paused in the doorway, acidly. 'How agreeable you are of a sudden, Miss Kingsley! I'll pick you up in ten minutes at the staff entrance. You'd better be there.'

She was there, knowing too well that he would never tolerate being kept waiting, and suddenly wary of the uncertainty of his moods. She didn't like him, nor could she imagine she ever would, but when she let him see her antagonism she found the subsequent sharpness of his tongue strangely upsetting.

This evening he drove himself and obligingly stopped his car in Moorland Road, but declined Celia's polite invitation to come in, asserting that he would rather wait outside.

Lucy hadn't yet returned, but Robin was home and told Celia that he thought Lucy had gone straight out with Denis after work, as usual. He was himself, so he assured her, going on to his club, and was more than pleased that she was off to see Timmy. He even offered to help gather her things together, and when she refused went on drinking tea and studying his evening paper without further comment. As if it was the most natural thing in the world for her to be going to Cheverly!

When they arrived at Cheverly Celia was damp merely from running into the house from the car, and, not waiting to call Mrs Timpson, Guy whipped her straight upstairs to her room. It was the same one she had occupied previously, and she was surprised to find the bed already made up and turned down for the night.

'I rang Mrs Timpson before we left,' Guy explained

smoothly, obviously interpreting the flicker of surprise on Celia's face. 'She knows you're coming. I expect she heard us arrive, but as usual she'll be busy.'

'Oh yes. Yes, of course,' Celia murmured, staring at him with a peculiar confusion as he put down her case but seemed disposed to linger.

His eyes swept the room as if to reassure himself that she had everything she might need, his gaze lingering thoughtfully on the pretty pastel sheets before coming back to meet her own. 'If you want anything,' he said, with cool politeness, 'Mrs Timpson will get it for you.'

'Thank you,' she replied, very formally, like a well brought up child, while a sharp shiver ran through her.

'You're cold?' he stepped nearer, his fingers raised to brush a crystal raindrop from her cheek. 'Take a hot bath,' he advised with a slight smile, 'dinner won't be until eight, which should allow you plenty of time.' His hand lingered gently for another heart-stopping moment, before he turned abruptly closing the door quickly behind him, leaving her standing, scarcely able to realise he had gone.

Celia had hastily pushed into an overnight bag a soft, creamy-white dress, belted with a silver buckle over a gently gathered skirt. With it she had included soft silver slippers which strapped around her ankles. But while feeling comfortable these distracted from her height, making her feel unnaturally small and vulnerable.

Carelessly she brushed out her still damp hair, which her prolonged immersion in a hot bath hadn't helped. She saw, to her sudden dismay, that it had grown too long, and catching a glimpse of herself in the mirror through the thick strands of it, she decided she looked entirely wanton and rigorously arranged it in her more usual chignon. If Guy had thought her appearance suggestive in the shop then she must give him no further cause for complaint.

There was within her a half conscious desire to linger over her dressing, but despite her deliberate lack of haste Celia was ready long before the prescribed hour. Too rest-

110

less to remain in her room, she ran down to the kitchen where she hoped to find Timmy. She had no wish to see Guy—not yet. Not until she had inviegled a little of Timmy's sanity. But she might have guessed that Mrs Timpson would be too busy.

'Oh, not now, my dear!' Despairingly she threw up her hands in her most emphatic manner. 'I can't possibly risk ruining Mr Ryland's dinner! We can talk later.'

Celia sniffed, appreciative if a little put out. 'Whatever it is, Timmy darling, it smells delicious. You'll have him thoroughly spoilt.'

'Oh, there you go again,' Mrs Timpson said disapprovingly, as a pan boiled over. 'Please take yourself out of here with your trying remarks. Be a good girl and I'll see you later.' And softly, as Celia pulled a not very impressed face and turned away, 'Some men are worth the spoiling.'

Forlornly Celia did as she was told, wandering back to the hall, and as there was no one here, she went into the drawing room. She found Guy Ryland standing before the fire with a drink in his hand.

Without asking he poured her a sherry. 'Cheers,' he nodded abstractedly, raising his glass briefly, his mind obviously on other things.

Slowly Celia took her drink to a nearby chair and sat down, very much aware of his presence even though he apparently chose to forget hers. A faint tremor of indignation stirred. Of her jeans and shirt he had been critical, but had no word of approval to spare for the extra effort she had made now. Recalling Timmy's remark, she thought they could both have wasted their time!

Yet his own appearance was always immaculate, she had to admit; something he seemed to achieve even when dressed casually, as he had done over Christmas. Celia glanced at him surreptitiously from under her beautifully mascaraed lashes. This evening he wore a fine, dark grey lounge suit with a blue silk tie, an outfit which enhanced his considerable good looks. His dark hair was well cut and

111

thick, slightly curling where it struggled against the discipline of the hairbrush, and self-assurance showed itself in the set of his broad shoulders. She felt her breath hurt somewhere deep down in her throat. All her life she would remember this moment, when it seemed she was seeing him for the first time.

His eyes suddenly moved over her, and her heart jolted as she felt their impact right through her body. 'After dinner,' he told her, seemingly conscious of her inquiring glance, 'we shall get down to business, but I like to have this half-hour. It relaxes the mind.'

Which clearly, Celia would have sworn, had been much preoccupied with something, if not business. Perhaps—she knew a slight coldness—perhaps Miss Morrison qualified as a deserving target for those obviously all-absorbing thoughts?

Indifferently, Celia tried to shrug. Apparently Guy expected no answer and as the gong sounded, he took her through to the dining-room where she remained strangely silent, disregarding his occasionally raised eyebrows which she pretended not to see throughout the meal. He hadn't, after all, asked her here for entertainment purposes, so he couldn't complain if she allowed her brain to rest as he did. He wasn't to know the neat little speeches she constantly rehearsed in her head; her introductory lines about Lucy and Denis which she knew well were too important to bungle.

But it wasn't about Lucy that they talked while drinking their coffee after dinner. It was about the fashion show that they were holding, and although Celia was surprised, she supposed it was all part of the business which he wished to discuss. 'It's all arranged,' she assured him when he asked. 'I believe it will go smoothly.'

'Something of a new innovation,' Guy's eyes narrowed thoughtfully, 'but one which I think will be well received, especially as you're to help with the modelling.'

As it's for charity I couldn't very well refuse,' she shot

back, wondering why she should feel so defensive. Perhaps if she concentrated on the veracity of his words she could ignore the underlying mockery, which seemed to imply ridiculously that to model a gown was something less than respectable! Yet how could he think this when even now he was holding Spring shows in most of the store's branches, and had been more than gratified by their success. 'It's scarcely a new innovation,' she pointed out dryly, 'and as you approve of it elsewhere, don't you think it would be a good idea to do a few more shows for the benefit of the store? Women are often much more eager to buy an outfit if they can study it first on someone else.'

'I suppose it could be considered,' he agreed, but with obvious reluctance. 'At any rate we can keep it in mind—for the future.'

Celia tried to smile naturally. 'But you asked me ... at least, you said,' she stumbled, 'that you wanted to engage me for this particular purpose?'

'Agreed,' he replied suavely, his eyes coolly assessing her perfect figure as if to punish her a little for an irritating tenaciousness, 'but with, as I've just said, an eye to the future. A great deal is yet to be done in the shop before we're ready to advance on this scale.'

Good heavens! He talked as though they were a corner shop without so much as the room to turn around. Which was mystifying when their present programme of alterations was being carried out so carefully as to scarcely affect anything at all. Frowning, she stared at him, as if trying to read what was on his mind, but found it impossible. There was nothing to be ascertained from the provoking smoothness of his face as he blandly regarded her inner perplexity.

Before she could find a suitable comment, he advised, 'Don't trouble yourself so much about things you have no time for at present. Do this charity show by all means, I intend to watch it myself. But I won't have you wearing yourself out. Now there's this business of the top floor.'

For an hour they discussed it and again Celia's intelli-

113

gence seemed partly obscured by bewilderment, as much that Guy talked about seemed away beyond her province, and she wondered rather desperately, not for the first time, what it was really all about. When Mrs Timpson came in to say goodnight she was momentarily startled. Although she welcomed the diversion, she hadn't realised it was so late.

'It's only just after ten,' Mrs Timpson smiled, 'but I've had a cold and I feel rather tired. I'll see you in the morning, dear, before you go.'

Accusingly, as the door closed, Celia looked at Guy Ryland. 'You never told me!'

'She wouldn't allow it,' he said, his tone implying that he refused to be taken to task about such an irrelevant detail. 'As she says, you can always see her in the morning. I won't be going back to Manchester until after lunch. You can consider you have the morning off.'

'Oh, but I couldn't!' Celia almost gasped, her heart giving a great lunge of protest. 'I mean, there's a lot to do and my immediate colleagues will wonder where I am.'

'I'll ring and tell them.' His voice sounded a lot cooler than her hot cheeks, and his dark eyes pinned her wide, startled ones emphatically.

'But I don't want you to ring and tell them anything! I just don't want to be late!' The accelerated beat of her heart forced her to further protest in spite of the authority in Guy's expression. Why should people be provided with something to talk about at her expense? A shop could so often be like a large family, with everyone knowing each other's business, and what they didn't know they made up. There'd been speculation enough about her reappearance at the store, Celia knew. She wasn't keen to arouse any more. All she wanted, she tried to convince herself blindly, was the chance to settle down and sort out her domestic affairs in private without any interference from anyone, least of all a man like Guy Ryland!

CHAPTER SEVEN

CELIA watched now as he rose leisurely to his feet, ignoring what she said as he glanced down into her over-bright eyes. 'Do you mind,' he asked, 'if I hear the news? There's something of particular interest.'

As she nodded mutinously he switched on the large colour TV set in the corner. 'Do you watch a lot?' he queried politely, coming this time to sit beside her on the settee where he might face the screen, and she was aware that he found her temper amusing and refused to pander to it.

'We don't have one,' she muttered, which was nothing less than the truth. Then, because she hated his indifference and suddenly had an urgent desire to escape, she said sharply, 'While you're viewing might I use your telephone, please? I did promise Lucy I would have coffee with her in the morning, and she won't know I shan't be in until later.'

'Robin does.' The reply was brief and tinged with impatience as he attempted to hear the outcome of a union dispute. 'I mentioned it was a possibility and no doubt he'll tell your sister.'

Your sister! Robin's sister! Never *Lucy*, unless he had no other alternative. Celia stared at the television set blindly, seeing nothing of the picture as she cried recklessly, forgetful of her former resolve to be cautious, 'I know you don't care for my sister, but she does have a name, and I don't see why you should object to the friendship between her and your cousin.'

Although she was looking away from Guy Ryland she felt him stiffen slightly. 'I wasn't aware that she and my—er—cousin were very great friends, if that's what you imply?'

'Not so great perhaps as yourself and Greta Morrison!' Celia taunted wildly, stung to sheer folly.

Which could all add up,' he replied, with derisive carelessness, 'to a complete set of illusions. It's remarkable the importance women can attach to that which might not even exist.'

She deplored the way he talked in riddles. Was he referring to himself or Denis and Lucy? She turned her glossy head slightly to glance at him, her breath coming far from evenly. 'You'll be telling me next,' she retorted, 'there's nothing between Greta and yourself!'

His eyes glinted and now she had all his attention as he abruptly switched off the television. 'If you're attaching a question mark to the end of that impertinent little sentence, my dear Celia, then I refuse to alleviate your curiosity.'

'You couldn't deny it,' she challenged unwisely as he sat once more beside her. The chin which she tilted defiantly was far from steady, and through her rapidly beating pulse she had the peculiar feeling that the conversation was swiftly moving from her control. Yet none of this seemed able to act as a brake for her impulsiveness. Not for one moment did she stop to ask herself how any affair Guy might be having with Greta could possibly have any bearing on Lucy's friendship with Denis.

Guy was taking his time in answering and the slight smile which edged his firm lips promised no kind of tolerance. 'Why should I trouble to deny anything?' he asked softly, watching her enigmatically. 'You must surely have indulged in the occasional affair yourself?'

An affair! His words were insulting and his tone more so, and his glance as it went over her left not a stone unturned. 'But of course,' she agreed in a most reprehensible fashion, scarcely realising in her utter indignation what she was saying. 'I'm not entirely naïve, Mr Ryland.'

His voice came with a hint of warning gentleness which, in his case, could be so wholly deceptive. 'Don't you think it's high time you stopped calling me Mr Ryland, Celia?'

116

Celia blinked, thrown slightly off course, the sudden flicker of her lashes betraying an inner uncertainty. 'You can't make me,' she muttered.

'Come here,' he exclaimed, unused to opposition of any kind, and not willing any longer to put up with hers. His steely grip encircled her waist, stopping her instinctive retreat, yet his voice was still soft, kinder than his hands seemed disposed to be on her narrow rib cage. His eyes on her startled face, he added sardonically, 'That beautiful head of yours is full of the strangest ideas. Why do you feel it necessary to fight me every inch of the way?'

Momentarily Celia went numb, her eyes widening as though with shock, the pupils dilated to a misty blueness as she stared up at him, held prisoner as much by something within herself as by the strength of his arms. The unexpectedness of Guy's action had taken her by surprise. The cool flick of his temper had not been unexpected because she had knowingly provoked it—but this!

'Why do you have to keep on fighting me?' he repeated, prompting keenly when she made no reply.

'I think we both know the answer to that one,' she cried.

She felt his body go taut and saw the expression in his eyes change as they looked down into hers. 'Our answers would be in no way identical, I'm thinking.'

His eyes mocked deliberately. Celia was aware of this, and unable to withstand such narrowed speculation she tried to turn her face away, wishing only to be free of him, of the wholly disturbing flame which his nearness ignited inside her. There was no logical explanation for a lot of things, not least the traitorous and entirely unpredictable reactions of her own body.

'Please,' she almost begged, her throat tight, 'you've had your little joke. You can't really enjoy treating me like this.'

'Oh, but I do,' his mouth twisted as he laughed softly. 'I find you quite enchanting, irresistibly so when you forget to be Celia Kingsley.'

'What do you mean?' she spluttered wildly.

117

But she was not to be answered with mere words. As if Guy had decided he had wasted too much time already, his hands tightened and his arms were hard as he pulled her ruthlessly closer, holding her gently but quite firmly with the weight of his body. Celia tensed, resisting him, knowing that if he kissed her she would be lost, but his fingers came unyielding beneath her chin and his lips, when they came down on her quivering ones, hurt.

He had held her in his arms before, but only carelessly, as if she had merely provided a brief diversion, not to be taken seriously. This was something different. Even though completely lacking in the experience she had so unwisely boasted of, Celia knew this. Now, after the first few moments of insistent exploration, he turned relentlessly on the soft sofa, jerking her down to him with so much force as to render impossible any resistance, and kissed her again and again with a rising passion.

Celia's struggles as he continued to kiss her lessened, and, as her own desire mounted to match his, she experienced again the vibrant, startling excitement which had almost frightened her at Christmas. This time, although her heart throbbed frantically, some part of her appeared to come awake with an almost triumphant pleasure, as if rejoicing to be rid for ever of those protective defences which, until she had met Guy Ryland, had rejected any such attack on her emotions. Her body, as she had thought she had known it, ceased to exist. There was only Guy; the hard, punishing strength of him, his mouth, which forced from hers a response such as she had never before imagined.

Then, as the tumult within her mounted to an unbearable tension, there came some instinctive rejection of complete domination. Wildly illogical, considering the sweeping force of her aroused emotions, her slight body stiffened, guided more perhaps by the last feeble remnants of innocence than by any genuine hope of survival. 'Guy,' she whispered faintly, her breath mingling with his as she tried unconsciously to escape him.

'Don't ...' His exclamation was low, but it sounded like a warning, an indication that he was in no way willing to pander to any pleas for leniency. 'Darling,' he murmured, lifting his hard mouth fractionally from her bruised lips, 'be still. You know I want you.' He murmured something else, scarcely audible this time, his mouth moving again against her hot skin, his hands caressing on the pliant softness of her body.

It was then that all desire to fight him faded and her arms, seemingly of their own accord, went up around his neck, her fingers with an urgency of their own curling on his strong shoulders, clinging with renewed pressure. 'Guy, oh, Guy,' she breathed, her voice aflame with longing, a shameless, half-conscious offering of herself.

That she had moaned his name without realising it was something she was barely aware of, but the subtle yearning in the way she said it was at once something different. It brought his eyes to her flushed face almost sharply, and there was more than a hint of victory in the lips which crushed hers again, forcing the last remaining strength out of her. His sheer masculine vitality was something she couldn't fight even had she wanted to, and at that moment with the wildness of delight running through her there was no desire anywhere inside her ever to be free of the arms which provided it.

Feeling now such intense response, Guy pulled her closer, holding her intently as she clung trembling, seeking as if to gauge the exact degree of her abandonment. His mouth slid from her cheek to her lips, his hands on her body sensuously demanding. His lips persuaded as he held her possessively to him again, pulsating with the hard masculinity which was so much a part of him, his hands sure and warm. Against her throbbing, blindly responsive mouth he whispered words of low reassurance which were in no way reassuring at all, but a dire threat, had she but realised, to any small breath of sanity she might still retain.

From that time onwards Celia stopped belonging to

119

herself. She could feel her heart fluttering, intoxicated with sensations which threatened to overwhelm her. Beneath the passion of Guy's touch she became alive, sobbing a little as she repeatedly murmured his name and pressed her aching body closer, wanting only that he should hold her and love her.

There seemed no sense at all when suddenly he straightened, almost wrenching her arms from about his neck, his face set as he slowly drew away from her, his hands falling to his sides. 'I think,' he said, looking at her for a long while, 'we could both do with a drink.'

'A drink!' Completely disorganised, wanting only to be loved, Celia stared at him as if bereft. Her hair, loosened from its usual tight knot, spilled about her rose-flushed cheeks and her eyes were shining with the depth of her newly aroused feelings. A drink was not what she wanted! Maybe it was what she needed, which was quite another thing. There lay in the hazy confusion of her mind the crazy conviction that she had been cheated. 'I don't want anything to drink,' she whispered, stumbling to her feet like someone in a trance.

Scarcely aware of what she was doing, she rose and stood beside him. 'Guy ...' her voice came strangely bleak, uncertain, her face full of a pleading apprehension. She knew an urgent longing to find the right words to express the turmoil that raged within her, yet none would come. The hand she laid tentatively on his arm trembled, as if she was aware that he was quite prepared to fling anything she might offer straight back at her again.

But the man's face was curiously empty, his eyes watchful, narrowed, the change in him wholly confusing. 'What is it you want so much, Celia?' His voice unnerved her, shocking by its extreme coolness. 'Once you've made up your mind we might be able to do something about it, but right now I don't feel in the position to do one damned thing.'

She shrank back as though he had hit her, the coldness in him bringing back sanity, if not enough to bring her completely to her senses. 'You can't just forget about me like this,' she cried, in no way conscious of what she was saying, driven, it seemed, by something stronger than herself.

'It would be madness!' As if talking to himself but goaded beyond immediate control, he suddenly jerked her to him. Catching a handful of her loose hair, he pulled her into his arms again and kissed her so hard she was breathless when he let her go. This time there was passion in his touch but no tenderness, as if her begging had in some way infuriated him. This, while bringing a wild regret, brought also a life-saving flood of cold reaction. As his arms slackened, an icy resentment cleared the drugged recesses of her mind, enabling her to pull herself free from his grasp and run with silent feet from the room.

'Celia!'

She heard him call abruptly after her, but the hard authority in his voice angered her and spurred her on to escape. To leave him while she still had the sensible inclination to do so, not daring to risk making a fool of herself twice in the same evening.

Visibly she shuddered with humiliation, her thoughts chaotic as she rushed upstairs to her room. Afterwards she never even remembered getting into bed after slipping a thin negligée over her tormented head. Her toilet was a scanty affair performed merely from habit, a dab of cold cream on her cheeks, a careless comb through her hair.

Both mentally and physically she felt exhausted, and prey to increasingly despairing thoughts. In Guy's study she felt she had been battered by elements which she had had no experience to help her cope with, and that she had finished up by making an almost complete fool of herself. She couldn't think what had come over her. She didn't know how she would ever forget.

Half sobbing with a desperate desire to escape such thoughts, Celia longed for the oblivion of sleep. Sleep, however, proved elusive and refused to oblige, and she felt the beginnings of a blinding headache. Thinking she would

121

have given almost anything for a hot drink, she was aghast when her door opened and Guy stood there with one in his hand.

As a purely involuntary act she smoothed back her tumbled hair, and with the back of the same hand scrubbed a betraying tear from hot cheeks, staring at him with open hostility. The dislike in her eyes was plain, she hoped, for him to see. 'I would just like,' she choked indistinctly, 'to be left alone!'

'Don't worry,' he assured her, with a mildness she so fervently envied, 'I merely brought you this. You declined before, but you look as if you might need it now.'

It was so clearly what she had longed for that her eyes fastened on it almost greedily, yet when he walked over and placed it with a couple of aspirin on her bedside table she couldn't find a word of thanks.

He glanced down at her, with a return of something like his usual impatience, taking in the apprehensive shape of her huddled under the tumbled sheets. 'You reminded me so vividly of a small, scared cat, I felt impelled to come and reassure you. You have nothing to be afraid of.'

Her head ached so blindly as to dull all other emotion but pain, enabling her to look at him with scarcely a tremor. 'I should never be afraid of you,' she replied coldly, and with what she was convinced at that moment was a modicum of truth.

He seemed prepared to accept this, although his eyes glinted as they rested thoughtfully on a single tear which channelled a lonely path through the smear of cream on her pale cheek. She looked about ten years old, and just as vulnerable. 'Goodnight, child,' he murmured mockingly, yet with a kind of subdued violence as he turned towards the door.

Next morning at breakfast, without preamble, Guy asked if she had slept well.

'Yes, thank you.' She contrived not to look at him while

122

he poured her coffee. It was winter, and this morning he wore a checked shirt of fine wool, open at the neck, showing the strong line of his throat. In spite of herself Celia remembered and shivered.

She quivered even more when he retorted dryly, 'You are indeed fortunate, even if you don't seem particularly rested. Maybe although you think you slept, you had bad dreams, and unfortunately your tossing and turning did little to ensure a good night's sleep for me.'

Carefully she concentrated on the lean strength of his wrist as he reached reflectively for more toast. She felt the colour which it seemed he could so easily arouse burning her smooth skin. How could he have heard? In a house as old as this were the walls really so thin? If so, why hadn't he put her in another room? 'I'm sorry,' she said at last, 'if I disturbed you.'

'Never mind,' he said briefly, his eyes meeting hers sardonically. 'We can always see what today brings.' He finished buttering his toast and picked up the morning paper. His temper seemed improved, but Celia fancied there was much that he had left unsaid.

She stared blindly at the back of the newsprint which danced strangely before her eyes, a fine slither of hate where her heart had been. Her mind, after an almost sleepless night, seemed not particularly endowed with clarity, but one thing she resolved with determination. She must refuse to have anything more to do with Guy Ryland! If they were both out for revenge because of the past, then she was prepared to admit he could be some way ahead, and every nerve in her body warned her to retreat. In the process there might be some damage to her pride, but if that were all what was a little lost pride, if otherwise she might remain intact?

As questions and answers buzzed dramatically through her head it seemed inevitable that Guy should suddenly lower his paper and find her wide-eyed gaze fixed on him, her thoughts too transparent to be anything else but completely readable. Her cheeks, flushing pink, clearly proclaimed her guilt, and it was obvious from the sudden tightening of his mouth that he used considerable restraint in refraining from some derisive comment. Instead he satisfied himself with a grimly ironic smile and a smooth query as to what she felt inclined to do that morning. Almost as if she were on holiday!

'I wondered,' he mused, 'if you would care to go walking, as we did at Christmas. I think some fresh air would do you good, and I could go with you.'

'Walking?' Celia drew a swiftly startled breath, too wary of her own vulnerability to do anything but protest. 'I thought we were here to work?' This morning she felt unable to even look at him without embarrassment, and the idea of strolling with him around his grounds was something she would rather not contemplate. 'I think,' she commented primly, 'I'd rather do something more constructive.'

He sighed, obviously again guessing her thoughts, and regretting that she hadn't the necessary sophistication to consider an hour of indiscretion as indifferently as he did himself. 'One of the advantages of being one's own boss, Celia, is that I can play truant occasionally—when the opportunity presents itself.'

'Which is probably too often,' she retorted coolly, adding quite irrationally, considering who he was, 'If one neglects a business it can never be a success.'

He grinned, where she might have expected him to be merely irritated by such a trite remark. 'I manage factories and a chain of retail stores. I can assure you they're too well established to collapse under the amount of neglect I was contemplating this morning.'

She stared at him, determined still to resist him in spite of his amused reassurance. Like a fractious child she felt a need to quarrel, and searched in her mind for another topic which might succeed in annoying. Inspiration arrived, although afterwards she felt some shame in using it. 'Lucy was telling me,' she began, in this instance quite truthfully, 'that Denis is keener on factory management than his work at the shop.'

'Maybe.' Guy Ryland shrugged without obvious interest, refusing to be drawn.

'Don't you think . . .' she continued.

'Celia!' Provoked at last, his eyes narrowed with exasperation. 'Denis Ryland might be considered a relatively bright young man, but he hasn't the first idea about production technology, nor production management if it comes to that. What exactly,' he asked with a fine sarcasm, 'had he in mind?'

'Surely,' she persisted, 'he could train for one or the other?'

'Too late,' he asserted, apparently not prepared to argue. 'Industrial technology—the actual machinery of a firm, the design and selection of technical equipment and its use—takes years of close study. As does production management, which as you should know is concerned with the people who actually use the machinery. It involves the planning and control of a firm—its human and financial aspects. Both of these branches are away beyond Denis's present capabilities, which might be something for you to remember when you try to play fairy godmother.'

All thoughts of a walk could now be rejected with an appropriate show of indignation. 'If you'll excuse me,' she exclaimed, jumping to her feet, 'I think I'll and see Mrs Timpson!'

'Yes, do . . .' she heard him agreeing as she turned away, the coolness in his voice a clear indication that her deliberate little tantrum didn't fool him for one minute, but he made no attempt to stop her or to renew his former invitation about a walk.

Celia spent the remainder of the morning with Mrs Timpson, not somehow trusting herself to go near Guy Ryland. She had no idea what he was doing, but eventually they heard him go out, and later, when the telephone rang, he informed Mrs Timpson that he was in Manchester

125

and would send a car for Celia after lunch.

Celia, almost bristling with temper at such high-handed-ness, cried, 'I could have gone with him! He knew I wasn't happy about missing work! Why ever did he go off like that?'

'You tell me, dear,' Mrs Timpson, not entirely unaware of the strained atmosphere, shrugged with some forbear-ance. 'Mr Guy usually has his reasons, which is more than I can say for others,' she added pointedly.

'I could always catch a bus,' Celia said sulkily, seeing no reason why Timmy should automatically assume she was to blame, and felt not at all pleased when the woman replied quickly, if with more patience, 'I shouldn't advise it, dear. Not in this weather, and the service is extremely bad.'

So Celia waited, simmering with a righteous indignation which Mrs Timpson wouldn't allow her to express, until after two o'clock when the car arrived for her. That Guy hadn't been pleased with her response last night or her remarks this morning was quite clear; this no doubt being his subtle way of demonstrating his disapproval. The com-plicated rehearsal in Celia's mind as to what she was going to say to him immediately she reached Manchester con-tinued throughout the journey.

But once at the shop, her temper subsided weakly as if his cool influence sought out and enclosed her, and she decided wearily against another confrontation. Nor did it seem that he was in any great hurry to see her, as she caught neither sight nor sound of him during the rest of the afternoon. A fact which should have cheered but strangely did not! Altogether, she mused, as she went home later, it had been a rotten day.

Robin said when he came in that Guy had gone away for a couple of days. He sounded extremely cheerful, as if it was something of a relief, and when challenged outright he agreed. 'I can't really relax when he's breathing down my neck all the time,' he confessed ruefully. 'I don't know where he gets his energy from, but I couldn't get through the half of what he does.'

'It's merely a matter of organisation,' Celia derided shortly, wondering why the weekend in front of her should stretch so bleakly into monotonous space.

'By the way,' Robin went on, apparently not noticing how Celia had gone suddenly pale, 'Lucy and Denis would like us to lunch with them tomorrow. I can't think why.'

Celia stared at him, momentarily silent with surprise.

'Don't ask me,' he shrugged carelessly, aware of the unspoken question in her eyes. 'Actually, it was Denis who insisted, and because it looks as if he'll eventually become one of the family, I agreed—for both of us. I hope I did right?'

'Probably,' Celia reluctantly conceded, continuing after a moment, with some bewilderment, 'I thought you were desperate to discourage their friendship?'

'Only because of Guy. This weekend he's out of the way.'

Within Celia a flicker of impatience flared. 'It's impossible to believe you're as stupid as all that, Robin! He'll be back—and I can tell you here and now that he's no more prepared to accept Lucy than ever he was. Last night he was annoyed when I so much as mentioned her.'

'Oh, dear,' Robin exclaimed, with his usual air of helplessness, 'oh, dear!'

But despite a returning apprehension, Celia decided in the end, it might be a good idea to accept Denis Ryland's invitation, if only because it might afford a chance to know him better. At Christmas she hadn't found herself able to like him very much, but first impressions, she knew, could be wrong. To get to know him away from the immediate vicinity of Cheverly might be to see him in a new light. In judging him as a young man somewhat lacking in sensitivity, she could have been wrong. Not all Rylands, she argued with herself, could be alike!

Denis informed them when he met them that he had booked their meal at a country pub he knew beside Lancaster, the county town, and for a little while Celia felt relieved to get away from the immediate vicinity of Manchester and didn't pause to wonder why Denis, on such a wintry day, should choose to go so far. Lucy, for once, seemed in such a good mood that Celia was loath to disturb it by protesting that she had hoped to escape after an hour or two in order to do some very necessary household shopping.

Denis drove a super sports car which positively ate up the miles, in a way which normally would have made Celia feel cheated of time to study the scenery, but today speed seemed contrarily to relieve the restless ache in her heart. They travelled along the M6 with its miles of sandy coastline to the east, and to the west the wild moorland country which, from its higher hills, afforded such magnificent views. The hills, interspersed with beautiful river valleys and wooded dales, were very familiar.

Nostalgia gripped Celia hard as they passed. So well she remembered the rugged fells which rose to the Pennine Chain and the border with north Yorkshire. She had done a lot of walking once, along the old traders' routes across the fells. Her father had been fond of taking them when they had all been younger, he himself being much more of a naturalist and a dreamer than the hard-headed business man he should have been. How many times had he shown them something of the wild life to be found in the hills. The oblivious, yet nervous rabbit, the fox and the deer. The hovering hawk; the heron, knee-deep in a tumbling beck.

What was there about other days, other times? Wistfully Celia sighed as they drove into Lancaster.

The pub to which Denis took them was comfortable but by no means the last word in luxury. 'All I can afford, I'm afraid,' he remarked, with no lack of candour as they entered the premises and sat down. 'Guy isn't exactly the last word when it comes to generosity.'

Somewhat startled, Celia glanced at him. She did have a rough idea what his salary would be, and unless Guy deliberately underpaid him he couldn't be as badly off as he made out. And why bring Guy into it at all? Celia's frown deepened as she stared at him. They were, after all, only here because he had been so insistent!

But the fact that his guests embarrassment showed clearly on their faces didn't appear to deter Denis in the least. He seemed to derive a certain satisfaction from indulging in the slightly outrageous, even to quarrelling impatiently with Lucy throughout the meal, which did nothing to help the general atmosphere.

How could they care for each other? Celia wondered as she listened. Apart from sharing a host of acquaintances and friends they appeared to have little in common. Only once did Celia catch Lucy gazing at a too-talkative Denis with an absorption that might possibly be love.

Yet not such a love as she herself might have shared with Guy Ryland. Suddenly shrinking, Celia shivered, not knowing where the notion had come from. Swiftly she put it from her, along with the wistful longing which seemed to come with it. Such an emotion could only disguise the hate in her heart which she tried to convince herself she had always felt for him.

The pub, although not opulent, was pleasant, and the food, surprisingly in the face of Denis's disparaging remarks, was good. Afterwards they wandered around the town, which took its name from the old Roman camp, built beside the Lune on this site. It was an attractive place, and, in spite of a prevailing incompatibility, Celia enjoyed renewing her acquaintance with it. There was the medieval castle on Castle Hill, which dominated the grey old city below; the magnificent priory and parish church of St Mary, part of which dated back to Saxon times. There was a tree-lined quay to remind people of the days when Lancaster was a port, handling a bigger tonnage than Liverpool. In Meeting House Lane there was the Friends' Meeting House, dating from 1690, where George Whitefield had often preached, and further on they found the Ashton

Memorial, opened in 1909 in memory of the Williamson family who gave the town the fine parks in which the memorial stood.

Although the afternoons were beginning to grow longer, it was still winter and darkness soon crept in, bringing with it mist and a fine rain from the coast. The pleasures of exploring thus diminished, they returned to Manchester for a late tea.

'We really must have the place done up, Robin!' Celia heard Lucy grumble about the state of the decor for the first time since she had come home.

From the corner of her eye Celia noticed Robin's indifferent shrug as she departed to plug in the kettle. She also, with some indignation, heard Lucy add as she closed the drawing-room door, 'Can't Celia do anything about it?'

That, Celia summarised, controlling her wrath, was probably because Denis was with them. Otherwise Lucy seemed quite willing to ignore the state of the house, sometimes to the extent of being reluctant to help with even the small household chores which at least gave an impression of tidiness. Usually she contrived to avoid even the making of her own bed, leaving the execution of such boring tasks to Celia.

This, so far as Celia knew, was the first time Denis had been here, and he had only agreed to come in this afternoon because she had refused to allow him to do otherwise. He had strangely enough seemed almost as reluctant to stay as Lucy had been to have him, and perhaps because of this Celia had insisted, some devil of perversity urging her on when otherwise she might not have bothered. If they could be awkward, she decided, then so could she; it wasn't necessarily their prerogative. If she was supposed to be here to help solve family problems, she had to start somewhere!

Nothing, however, went according to plan. She returned with the tea-tray to find Denis yawning with an unconcealed boredom and an obvious inclination towards stirring things up a little. With a mischievous glance at Lucy he jumped up to help Celia with her tray, at the same time contriving to point out loudly and clearly that in his estimation Celia was a very attractive girl.

'You've seen me before, over Christmas,' she retorted mildly, conscious of Lucy's scowling face. She could have told Lucy that she only appreciated compliments from those whom she liked, and she wasn't even sure that Denis was sincere.

Before she could add any more, Denis laughed ironically, his eyes wandering with renewed appraisal over Celia's flawless beauty. 'I saw you, yes, but with old Guy around acting the watchdog I was forced to look the other way.'

'You're only trying to make me jealous, darling.' Lucy laughed in turn, if with little real mirth. 'I wonder if you know that Celia spent the night before last at Cheverly, so you'd better keep looking the other way.'

'He's simply teasing, darling,' Celia interceded quickly, slaying Denis Ryland with one glance. Hadn't Lucy noticed that Denis had been too busy looking at Greta at Christmas ever to notice her? He flirted with Greta Morrison, now he attempted to with Lucy's own sister. What on earth could Lucy see in such a man? And Lucy had had no right to mention she'd stayed at Cheverly! 'I only went to Cheverly,' she felt forced to explain to Denis's raised eyebrows, 'to visit Mrs Timpson who I expect you already know, used to look after us here before she went to Mr Ryland's mother.'

'Oh, I see ...' His dark face, which bore little resemblance to his cousin's, was bored again. 'Well,' he grinned after a moment's reflection, 'I'm willing to believe it. I can see that you would be a bit too innocent to appeal to a man of Guy's calibre. He likes 'em more—er—sophisticated, shall we say.'

More experienced, he means, Celia thought bitterly after he and Lucy had left. Her mind turned over with oddments of reflective confusion, but through it all came clearly the memory of Guy's kiss. In the silent reaches of her heart she whispered again and again, 'Oh, please, please, someone help me!'

Lucy and Denis, after having apparently buried their differences, had gone to see a film, and Robin, as usual, was away to his club. Celia, having declined to join either party, was after only half an hour regretting such a hasty decision. With a curious detachment she saw how she could scarcely bear to be alone with her thoughts, and the shock of such a revelation took its own toll. Long after midnight, after spending exhausting hours on housework in the hope of inducing sleep, she still lay awake, staring out through her window at a night so dark that she found it impossible to find even one tiny flicker of light.

CHAPTER EIGHT

GUY didn't return until the following Thursday and Celia was to remember his homecoming for quite a long time. In the meantime she took it upon herself to make several momentous decisions about the new alterations which she realised were directly contrary to Guy's plans. It might not be logical, but to act in such a way was the only antidote she could find to the urgent need within herself to re-establish on firmer ground her dwindling inclination to continue fighting him. Quite aware that the absurdity of at least one of her decisions would infuriate him to a degree, she waited, without hope of disappointment, for the cyclonic reaction she knew would come.

The chief architect, a lifelong acquaintance of Guy Ryland's, was mildly amused and not a little curious. 'Don't you think we should have waited until Guy returned?' he queried, looking, in spite of his smile, much more apprehensive than Celia considered necessary.

'Oh, what's one wall, one way or another?' she shrugged. 'Besides, Guy did leave me in charge.'

'Hm—well, so far as the wall is concerned, a couple of days, the work of a dozen men. No, I don't think he'll quibble if it has to come down again!'

'Well, you needn't be so sarcastic about it,' she muttered, feeling, though she tried to hide it, her first real tremor of fright. Had she been mad? Yet as Keith Cummings said, it was only one wall.

'Let's have some coffee, anyway.' Keith grinned in a way which he hoped might bring some colour back to Celia's paling face, coffee and a sympathetic demeanour being all he could truthfully think of at the moment. He had been gone himself for two days, following the unexpected death of a relation in the north of Scotland, otherwise he imagined this—he didn't like to call it a catastrophe —might have been averted. So far as the wall went, the original plan, the one Celia was working from, had been rejected by Guy as impractical. The pity of it was that they hadn't literally scrapped it. It had still been lying around, but he would have thought a girl of Celia's intelligence would have remembered.

For several minutes they were silent, drinking their coffee, each prey to an increasing uneasiness of mind. Celia felt tired, the result of too many sleepless nights, too much muddled longing for something beyond her reach. Her long nervous fingers, as they threaded through her tightly coiled hair, betrayed this, as did the faint lines of strain about her sensitively curved mouth. Yet the man watching saw only a slightly ruffled enchantment, a sensuously innocent attraction she seemed entirely unaware of. She looked very young and very graceful, her slender body curved to the back of a sleek office chair, almost as if she felt it was the only support she could count on.

'I must have been mad,' she said, repeating aloud what she had been thinking a moment ago.

133

'Not to worry,' he sighed, with some resignation. 'It probably doesn't make all that much difference either way. In fact,' he pondered, 'the way you've done it could be marginally better, looking at it from a woman's point of view.'

'You try telling Guy that!'

He disregarded the bitterness. 'He's not usually so obtuse. It depends,' he added enigmatically, 'it could depend, I mean, on which of the female sex he had in mind, his customers or you.'

'I can't think what you mean, Keith!' Celia exclaimed, able to speak to him without the peculiar restraint she always felt with Guy.

But Keith Cummings refused to be drawn further. There were some areas a man could be safer out of. 'I'm not exactly sure I can explain,' he hedged, draining the last of his coffee. 'A mere hunch is something I don't believe in airing too freely. Invariably I'm wrong.'

'And you can take it that this is no exception,' came a cool but utterly furious voice from the doorway. 'I should advise you to have your explanation ready, because I'm just about to demand one!'

The unexpectedness of Guy Ryland's arrival took both Keith and Celia by surprise, but if their initial reaction was similar, their subsequent degree of discomposure was entirely different. Keith, for some reason he couldn't fathom, did not feel as greatly disturbed as he might have done, but for Celia, to see Guy standing within a few feet of her seemed to spell out disaster in capital letters. Especially as he looked so completely infuriated!

Her breath rasping in her throat, she tried valiantly to speak before Keith Cummings. 'It was in no way Keith's fault,' she managed, not pretending to misunderstand what Guy was on about.

Guy, not one whit placated, whipped around on his architect, his face bleak. 'Then whose damn fault is it, then, if not yours? I return after a mere few days to find

134

the place a shambles, and the builder waving in front of me the wrong set of plans!'

'I'm trying to tell you ...' Again Celia intervened before Keith could get a word in. 'Keith has been away too. A close relative died. These things do happen. I accept all responsibility.'

Meeting her widening gaze, Guy's eyes reflected ice. 'What you're trying to tell me, Miss Kingsley, is that the wrong work is being carried out, on your orders?'

'I refuse to admit it's wrong,' she countered, her voice steadying, coming almost as coldly as his, 'but yes, the work which is being done was directly authorised by me.'

There followed this brief statement several long seconds of silence, fraught with an almost tangible tension which Keith Cummings found slightly unnerving. Never before had he seen Guy Ryland looking as if he would like to strangle someone—a girl at that—with his bare hands! He appeared to be finding it almost physically impossible to keep his hands off her. In fact, Keith surmised more accurately than he knew, if it hadn't been for his own presence he wouldn't like to have gambled too heavily on the outcome!

Feeling in this instance that silence wasn't so much golden as sheer folly, Keith said quickly, 'It's probably been a series of misunderstandings. I'm sure Celia means well, but I don't exonerate myself from all blame.'

'I'll see you later!' Without so much as glancing again in Keith's direction, and apparently intent now only to be rid of him, Guy waved towards the door, his gesture of dismissal unmistakable.

'Please go, Keith.' Celia joined her plea to Guy's as she saw Keith hesitate. 'I can assure you I can easily deal with this!'

Unhappily aware that both had forgotten him almost before he was out of the room, Keith went. Not because he hoped to escape unscathed—he didn't doubt Guy's word that he would see him later—but Celia's white face, in spite of rash bravado in her voice, was enough to make any man feel like the proverbial rat deserting a sinking ship.

Keith's impressions weren't so far wrong. Scarcely had the door closed behind him than Celia felt her arm grasped cruelly as she was thrust down again into the chair she had vacated only a second before with the vague hope that she would be in a stronger position on her own two feet.

Any such hope died a quietly natural death as Guy let go of her arm but still towered over her. If only he wasn't so powerful! She trembled as his words hurtled about her helpless head.

'Now,' he was saying, with a kind of savage sarcasm, 'if you would be so kind as to tell me exactly what has been going on, I'd be greatly obliged!'

It was much worse than Celia ever imagined it would be, but in the ensuing minutes while Guy stared down at her, obviously a man under considerable strain, she knew her only hope of survival lay not in cowardly appeasement but in standing up for her rights. After all, she did have some!

Borrowing from a reserve of strength she didn't know she possessed, she tilted her chin and retorted sharply, 'I really don't see what the fuss is all about. You did leave me in charge of this particular operation, and how many times have you stressed my management potentiality?'

'Which has, quite clearly, gone to your head! Endeavouring to induce a little confidence is not the same as bestowing unlimited power. Management potential can mean many things, Miss Kingsley. In your case it is, to a certain extent, quite applicable, but not as far as you've chosen to carry it out.'

Her cheeks bright pink, she glared at him. 'You ought to have drawn red lines!'

'Which will certainly be on my pad for reference in future—if there's to be any! Within your own capacity, and the training you've undertaken so far, you're excellent, but you were certainly quite unfit as yet for the decisions which you've obviously made with such relish while my back was turned!'

Her defence mechanism instinctive, Celia shrivelled, hugging her arms around herself as if to ward off a physical blow. To say Guy Ryland was furious would be putting it too mildly! She could feel his rage encompassing her, relegating her swiftly to a poor creature of no account, and his remark about her future filled her with apprehension, frightening because of its very intensity. She had been foolish, possibly stupidly so, and if he had been prepared to be more reasonable she might have apologised. In fact, she would have been only too willing to admit an obligation to do so, but not now. Never now! If he couldn't control his apparently uncontrollable temper, then wild horses wouldn't drag any sort of apology from her!

Afterwards Celia was to realise that to have grasped immediately the first opportunity to say she was sorry might have saved her limitless heartache. It also might have saved her from another kind of punishment which she shrank from remembering.

Guy's broad shoulders came between her and the light, leaving his face in darkness and giving him all the advantage as he stood waiting, his hard mouth ironic, for a suitable explanation. She was suddenly glad of the firm chair beneath her, and huddled to it closely. He asked for the impossible, something she wasn't prepared to give, but it wasn't easy to even think straight with a man like Guy Ryland breathing fire all over her!

With a desperate and if she had but known it, rather futile optimism, she attempted to change the subject. 'I hope you enjoyed your break,' she said.

His hand clenched, then closed over the vulnerable slope of her shoulder, his eyes deepening to black, with menace glittering in them. 'Don't tempt me too far, Miss Kingsley! I'll only take so much from you!'

Her nerves trembled as she wrenched back from his hands and it seemed as much as she could manage to keep her voice steady. 'I still don't see,' she retorted swiftly, 'why you're so upset. I've considered all along we could get better results from doing it—er——'

'Your way!' As her voice faltered in an unconscious search for words which she hoped would not antagonise him further, he supplied the obvious end to her defiant little sentence with open cynicism. 'Women must always have their own way, mustn't they? This is why they so often fail. They're singularly lacking in objectiveness.'

'That's unfair!' She looked very young and very haughty.

He went on cuttingly as if she had never spoken. 'The equality you so desperately strive for simply doesn't exist. Equality, as such, doesn't come into it. Women are so busy trying to give the impression of complete superiority that they'll go to any lengths to achieve it!'

Apprehensively she stared up at him, her eyes wide. 'But that's ridiculous, and you know it! I might as well accuse you of using your superior strength to push me into this chair. You didn't stop to consider whether I wanted to sit in it or not.'

Harsh sardonic humour leapt into his eyes. 'In another minute I'll not be responsible for what I do to you, Miss Kingsley. And I certainly won't stop to consider whether you're willing or not. We went over the final design for this particular department a dozen times. I have vastly the more experience, and against my better judgment and,' he added dryly, 'against the opinion of others whom I was quite aware thought I should know better, I've granted you concessions in plenty. And then what happens? Because I pandered stupidly to your whims you choose to imagine you could have it all your own way, and when my back is turned, to prove your point, you deliberately countermand my orders—to the cost of several thousands of pounds.'

'You must be mistaken!'

'At a rough estimate ...'

'But it wasn't like that at all! I mean ...' Again Celia's voice trailed off as her heavy lashes dropped despairingly

138

on to white cheeks. How could she possibly confess what had driven her to such lengths? He must know he was being unfair to women in general, but probably she herself was guilty of much he maintained. Hadn't she allowed her personal problems to become so mixed up with her business ones she couldn't think straight? Not any more! Men like Guy Ryland were in the enviable position of being able to leave their emotions at home. The more intimate ones, anyway. No such disruptive influence was ever allowed to intrude into their working lives.

His eyes gleamed now over every transparent line of her smooth young face with cool speculation. 'I'm waiting,' he prompted.

'I can only repeat what doesn't appear to please you,' she muttered inanely, brushing long tangled strands of thick tawny hair from off her lightly perspiring brow. Some part of her seemed torn between rage and tears while guilt hovered severely in the background. If only Guy didn't seem so completely alienated!

'I still think you exaggerate,' she said unwisely. 'If only you would try looking at the whole thing rationally, you would see I'm not so far wrong. And you can't really hold me responsible for what others choose to think. Besides, I doubt if anyone noticed anything. You probably just imagined it.'

'So.' His dark eyebrows shot up as he studied her for one formidable moment. 'My reasoning is at fault now? Do you think I particularly enjoy the speculation in the eyes of my staff when I follow you around—consult you on matters over the heads of my top men! Even now they're probably placing bets as to whether I'll be able to bring myself to sack you or not.'

'Dismiss me?' Celia felt her voice shake as she jumped to her feet, hearing only those two words clearly, uncomprehending of the rest of his speech. An irrational anger won hands down over the regret in her heart, stirring as it did an outraged sense of pride. Unable to sit still, she sprang up, a hectic colour tinting her pale skin. 'Well, you needn't bother, Mr Ryland, I'll save you the trouble. I'll go of my own accord, and quietly! After today,' she cried with a wild but totally satisfying recklessness, 'you won't ever see me again.'

'Oh no, you don't!' He came around the desk, the gleam in his eyes so full of menace that she retreated against the wall. He closed the gap between them, stopping within inches, and his hands came up on either side of her, cutting off any further line of escape. 'We made a bargain, my dear, and you're sticking to it. Don't think for a moment you're going to take the easy way out.'

'Now it's you who's being ridiculous!' Was it possible to speak clearly when one's heart was beating so hard it must surely be audible?

'My prerogative,' his voice cut grimly. 'I do happen to be your boss. And you'll stay here and more or less twiddle your thumbs until you're prepared to apologise.'

'Apologise!' The way she said it, she might not have known the word.

'I mean it!' His mouth was decisive. 'You can learn to crawl, Celia Kingsley. And if your dignity won't allow you to so much as bend, it might be a painful process.'

'I will never . . .' she began.

'Oh yes, you will,' he cut in forcibly, his voice not raised but dynamic. 'I've been too lenient in the past, I can see it now. You might have responded better to this sort of treatment.'

Before she could evade him his hands slid from the wall to pull her roughly to him. Too clearly he had only punishment in mind when he grasped her smooth chin with inflexible fingers and lowered his head to remove, without argument, the remaining breath from her body.

Caught completely off balance, Celia clutched at him to steady herself, prepared to struggle vigorously. Yet, when his lips touched hers, she went limp against him, sharply aware, as always, of the instant response within herself to his embrace. His lips hurt with the leashed anger behind them as he crushed her to his powerful frame. She could scarcely endure it, but his hand held her slender nape so that she was unable to move even one fraction, and all the time his hard mouth took a cruel revenge from her softly shaking lips. He was punishing her again and again, and to endure such a deliberate assault was to know a pain which in turn brought the beginnings of faintness. There seemed no mercy in him anywhere, and she couldn't believe any man could treat her in this way; yet despite his cruelty, her headlong physical response to him seemed to constitute by far the greater danger. It was too much, too sudden for her to cope with, and everything was fading strangely into darkness.

Then, just as swiftly as he had taken her, Guy let her go, and Celia shivered uncontrollably before the wholly calculating look in his eyes. Her body slumped, and she found the greatest difficulty in simply standing up. She thrust the back of her hand helplessly across her dazed forehead, seeking to brush away the fine mist which seemed to be obscuring her vision. There was a wild, almost impetuous clamour of words in her heart, but she could find absolutely no voice to express them.

Such restrictive influences, however, seemed in no way to control him. For several seconds he continued to survey her coolly. 'That's just a warning,' he said grimly, 'as to what might follow if you're not prepared to do things my way!'

Without another word he turned and walked out of the room, and without being conscious of how she got there, Celia found herself sitting at her desk, her aching head buried in her hands, a desolation in her heart which she was sure she would never survive.

It was no comfort either that for the remainder of the afternoon no one came near her. It seemed quite clear to her that everyone must be aware she was in Guy Ryland's black books, and, not surprisingly, no one dared sympathise. Besides, she would be seen to be obviously in the wrong. Her case would certainly not be helped by the fact that she had only been back at the store for a few short weeks and enjoyed a position which perhaps in some quarters had given rise to a certain amount of controversy. Celia was well aware that though she might be reasonably popular and respected, especially among the older staff, it was to a certain extent because she was Ronald Kingsley's daughter. In some quarters her possible downfall might be welcomed. Although she didn't flatter herself she was in any way more noteworthy than anyone else, she knew that there would be a great deal of head-shaking going on. It was Guy Ryland who had their total allegiance now—not a Kingsley—and there would be several who would not hesitate to let her know it!

How could she do anything else but hate a man who, by making his disapproval so publicly clear, had exposed her to so much idle speculation? During the dark hours which followed Celia decided emphatically that she would not go back to the store, no matter what Guy Ryland said or did. No one apparently cared what happened to her, neither Robin nor Lucy—nor Guy Ryland—so why should she bother what happened to any of them?

Robin, when he returned home that same evening after having heard something of what had happened through the usual grapevine, told her with brotherly candour that she was mad. 'You've had more concessions than anyone,' he grumbled. 'Certainly Guy might have had his reasons, but did you have to choose this particular way to throw it all back in his face?'

'You certainly have been busy!' Celia was furious, and welcomed the fury which seemed able to hide a conscious ache. 'One small incident blown up out of all proportion! And one,' she added more coldly, 'which ought to have been private between Guy Ryland and myself.'

'Oh, come off it, Celia,' he almost hooted with derision. 'I had nothing whatsoever to do with it! While Guy was away I might have offered advice—if you'd been prepared to listen—but the once or twice I tried you didn't hesitate to let me know that anything I had to say was unwelcome.'

'Why don't you say it, then?'

'Say what?'

'I told you so! Oh, Robin, don't look so glib! You've been longing to say that all week! And I quite realise you wouldn't personally start all this gossip, but I would like to know who did.'

Robin shrugged. 'Well, you know at the shop how it is. We're all one big happy family!'

'Sarcasm doesn't become you,' she muttered indifferently, 'I know how it is, but that still doesn't explain ... I don't think Guy Ryland would even condescend to discuss it with anyone.'

Again Robin laughed mockingly. 'I wouldn't say Guy was directly responsible, but indirectly—well, that's another thing. His confrontation with the builders wasn't exactly conducted in sign language, nor, I believe, was his subsequent interview with Keith Cummings.'

Fearing that to say more might only give the impression that she was attaching too much importance to her own part in the matter, Celia, with a supreme effort of willpower, pleaded with Robin to let the whole thing drop. But later, when Lucy came rushing home to pick up the tirade, she felt she had as much as she could take, and resolved again to return to London.

Why then, with her mind so adamantly made up, did she commit the extreme folly of walking back into the store next morning as if nothing had happened? The pride betrayed by the natural tilt of her small chin might have supplied the answer, and in her own mind it was absolutely the only reason she was there. She might run away from many things but never a Ryland, she had told herself firmly. And when her heart had quivered and faltered before such a blatant evasion of the truth, she tried to believe, as she had done on previous occasions, that it was simply because of her brother and sister. That she really had precious little choice!

Not that she had made it too easy for them. She had lain in bed until the chink of crockery and smell of burnt toast had drifted up from the kitchen, driving her reluctantly into action. The rather guilty relief on their faces when she appeared, dressed for work, had at least proved some sort of consolation. Another time she might even have been moved when Lucy placed in front of her a tentative offering of bacon and eggs. Usually nowadays the preparing and cooking of breakfast was left to Celia, otherwise there would never be any. Which had made it seem doubly regrettable that, considering the very special effort Lucy must have made, Celia was unable to eat it, her appetite being completely non-existent.

She didn't see Guy except from a distance for the rest of the week, and while he made no attempt to come near her she had the feeling that he still waited for an apology. She missed him, missing the habit he had begun to form of dropping into her office, of sharing her morning coffee while he consulted her on this and that. It was as if she had glided, buoyed up by his protective surveillance, only to have it abruptly taken from her. It was too sudden a deflation, like crashing down from the mountain tops, the hurt in her heart an almost physical part of her. Sometimes when she was alone an apology wavered on the edge of Celia's tongue, the urgency of it once carrying her as far as Guy's office door. Just in time she had stopped herself from knocking and going in, and had retreated furtively, thankful that no one appeared to have seen her.

But the pride which Celia hung on to with such stubborn determination did little to soothe the savage sickness in her breast. No long hours of work, which included detailed arrangements for the fashion parade, seemed to help much either. The dress show did, however, prove a welcome diversion, and intent on making a success of it, she gave it all her time and energy. Anything to shut out the memory

144

of Guy's derisive face and his humiliating kisses.

If she had decided there was nothing about a dress show to alarm her unduly, she was startled to find this was not so on the morning when Greta Morrison walked in.

'Guy sent me along to see if I could help,' the girl proclaimed, her smile containing a little glow of satisfaction. 'After all, it seems only fair that I should do something as I'm a member of the particular charity which is to benefit.'

'Guy——' Celia rejoined stupidly. 'You mean, Mr Ryland?'

'Of course!' Greta laughed with a little gay triumph, 'who else?'

Who else, indeed! Those two words, the way Greta said them, had a suffocating effect. 'I think,' Celia made an attempt to speak levelly, ignoring illogical pain, 'I think I have everything under control.'

'Guy wondered . . .'

Did he, indeed? Wild indignation swept aside Celia's despair. Already she had fallen down on one project, but it was fortunately something which could be hidden from the outside world. Now he had sent his girl-friend to make sure she didn't botch up a more public enterprise! Yet to be perfectly fair, Greta was attractive, and, if her style was a little flamboyant, on a platform she might do more than hold her own. 'Had you anything particularly in mind?' Celia asked, turning away to watch an eager assistant rehearsing in a pretty afternoon dress.

'I think the skirt is a little too long,' Greta spoke over her shoulder.

'Not really,' Celia spoke absently. 'The girl's not exactly right for it, that's all.'

'If you say so.' Greta made no attempt to hide a delicate yawn, losing interest as Celia told the girl to try on something else.

'I'd rather do evening wear,' Greta stated idly.

'You mean . . .?'

'You're rather dense this morning, darling, aren't you?

I mean I'd rather model something longer. I've been told I have quite a seductive figure.'

By Guy? Who else could it have been? Celia, remembering how his eyes had often examined hers closely, knew he noticed such things. She went hot. 'As you like, of course.' Refusing to be ruffled by her own thoughts, she agreed sweetly. 'Perhaps you would care to take a selection along and consult Mr Ryland himself. He might be only too pleased.'

Greta's laugh tinkled. 'I'd rather surprise him. Men do like a mystery, and enjoy being kept guessing.'

With unerring taste, which Celia could do nothing but admire, Greta chose a dress of black and amber, the bold stripes complementing her sultry beauty. There were also others which she put to one side until, alarmed by the growing pile of them, Celia was forced to protest that Greta couldn't do the whole show herself.

Greta merely laughed again and said she almost could, given half a chance, and for the next hour amused herself by trying on numerous gowns, very few of which fitted perfectly. Some of these she discarded, but the ones she liked she demanded to have altered, and she was not satisfied when Celia stressed that this wasn't possible in the time available.

'That one can be pinned or maybe tacked this evening, when you have it on,' she relented, sympathising, in spite of the bother she was causing, with the girl's disappointed face as she preened herself in a bright scarlet model. 'Most of these clothes must go back into stock.'

'Guy says he'll auction most of them at the end of the show, as his contribution towards our charity,' Greta informed her smugly, obviously realising that this was something Celia wasn't aware of. 'He's really rather a pet—when you get to know him. When you know how to manage him.'

'I wouldn't have thought so,' Celia said flatly, as she turned away crossly, resisting with difficulty a powerful

146

impulse to scream. How like him not to tell her, to place her in such an intolerable position!

After the show, Celia did know, there was to be a small private party at Guy's flat. Robin had told her, also the buyer who was responsible for most of the Spring clothes they were showing, but of course from Guy himself she had heard nothing.

'You're sure to get an invite, dear,' the buyer said, her voice warm with an aggravating sympathy. As if, Celia thought bitterly, she was quite informed regarding the strained relationship between Celia and the owner of the store!

'I happen to have an engagement after the show, I'm afraid,' Celia replied, with face-saving dishonesty, and immediately despised herself for 'sinning her soul' on account of Guy Ryland. She didn't have to invent a fictitious excuse, and one which might easily find its way back to him.

'We're all so very excited,' the woman gushed on. 'The heads of most of the departments are going, as well as some of the other personnel. You're sure to be there, dear,' she concluded with such emphasis as to make Celia realise that as far as excuses went she might well have saved her breath!

The day wore on, progressing, as such days invariably don't, with a remarkable smoothness, and the credit was mostly due, so it was whispered, in no small way to Celia's undoubted ability and her wholehearted dedication. On the night of the show all went well. Fortunately one of the restaurants was easily converted into a suitable auditorium, as there was a small raised dais at one end which had been built originally to accommodate a small orchestra, the only snag being the actual last-minute arranging of seats and regrouping of tables.

Half an hour before the show found Celia still in a pair of torn jeans belted tightly to her slim waist, with her newly-washed hair tied carelessly at her nape with a piece of rather tattered ribbon.

147

It was thus that Guy Ryland found her, sitting cross-legged on the floor with an electrician, adjusting lights. At least this was what Celia appeared to be engaged on, but Guy, approaching unnoticed, had the impression that the electrician's attention was more taken with the girl by his side. Guy dismissed him with a perfunctory wave of his hand, a hard compression to his mouth which should have made Celia wonder but didn't. Her heart was beating too uncomfortably, and the flex in her hand trembled, and everyone around them seemed to look as though they feared she and Guy were going to have another quarrel and wished they could fade away. Some did manage to take themselves off as far as possible with a show of tact which was in itself embarrassing, and effectively immobilised the beginnings of the glow of relief she had known when first she had caught sight of him standing there.

'What did you want?' she asked, so sharply that she instantly regretted using such a tone.

As if he gauged her mood and adjusted his own accordingly, his face hardened, and almost insolently his eyes lingered on the missing buttons of her shirt and travelled slowly down to the rent in her trousers. 'Do you have to make such a public exhibition of yourself?' he snapped curtly.

Celia blushed hotly, but, about to retaliate, she became aware of more than one pair of ears straining. 'We're busy,' she retorted, trying with effort to modulate her voice, 'you could call it working against the clock if you like, and help would be much more appreciated than criticism!'

'But I'm not criticising.' His tone was deceptively mild. 'I'm merely surprised that you choose to expose your—er—charms to all and sundry.'

Anger deepened the colour already in Celia's cheeks as she noticed his eyes, not nearly so indifferent as his voice, lingering on her untidy bodice. Yet she didn't seem able to move away from him and was conscious that his gaze, as his lips had done, aroused inside her an unnerving reaction.

Her breath caught as her eyes misted and he wavered before her. Desperately trying to hang on to a shaking equilibrium, she clasped her trembling arms tightly around herself, feeling her whole body tauten.

'Which doesn't help any,' Guy observed cryptically, 'especially if you're working against time. Actually,' he went on, returning deliberately to the more mundane, 'I came to see if everything is going according to plan. There are always last-minute snags.'

'Nothing I can't cope with, Mr Ryland.' Had his choice of words been accidental, or intentional? Could he possibly have chosen this moment to remind her of her former follies? 'I can assure you,' she exclaimed in stiff little undertones, 'that I don't make a mess of everything I do.'

He ignored this. 'After the show, Miss Kingsley, I'm holding a small party for some of the staff. Just a brief gesture of appreciation. I'm sure you would wish to be there.'

'Only if you really want me!' she cried, hating his phrasing, the words wrung from her before she could stop them. If she were asked to this party—and the chance had seemed remote—she had intended refusing immediately.

'Can you doubt it!' Sardonic as before, he deliberately mocked, his eyes again on the few remaining fastenings of her blouse. 'Just make sure you come, and I'll try to find time to be more explicit.'

'I don't know.' Blindly Celia shook her whirling head, feeling nothing but a kind of futile resistance. If only he would be kinder! She was suddenly relieved to catch the buyer waving wildly. 'I'd better go,' she said swiftly. 'I see I'm needed.'

'One moment.' His hand was on her arm detaining her. 'You're just compering the show, I understand?'

Startled, she glanced from his hand to his face. 'Well,' she was puzzled, 'not exactly. I'm a trained model.'

'Greta said you would merely be directing operations.'

'She's modelling quite a few of the gowns, so you needn't think I've fobbed her off with something unflattering. She's doing only the best.' Greta's name brought back the bitterness of disillusionment and she tugged away from him, her face white.

'I'm sure Greta will do nothing that isn't circumspect, but I don't want you parading in front of everyone!'

So he couldn't bear to see her stealing Greta's limelight, or maybe getting even a small share of adulation, after the crimes she had committed. 'Don't worry,' she taunted, 'I shan't let you down. Did you imagine I might use the audience to list your sins, Mr Ryland?' Which were much more excusable than the wildness of her words; this she knew, and she stared at him with a sinking heart.

'You little devil.' He eyed her grimly, his voice slightly clipped, but he said no more about the show. As if aware of where they were he let go of her arm and stepped back. 'I'll expect you after nine,' he said, every word a threat.

CHAPTER NINE

CELIA wasn't really surprised that although she had organised it and nearly worn herself out over it, she didn't enjoy the fashion parade one bit. She might have done, she told herself, but for the fact that Guy Ryland sat within a few feet of the stage and appeared to have his eye on her for most of the two hours the show ran. A watching brief, she supposed it would be called in some circumstances. He was now apparently so suspicious of her motives that he must keep her under constant observation, at least on such occasions as this, where his public image might once more be at stake! Greta, too, Celia noticed, came in for her share of attention, and confusingly Celia felt again the same hard twinge of pain she had known earlier when Guy had been concerned over the girl.

The event, as Celia had arranged it, proved an undoubted success, and while the proceeds of the evening would go to charity the firm would benefit as well, if only indirectly by way of advertisement. The huge restaurant was packed to capacity, and among the crowd were many of Guy Ryland's most influential friends. The room seemed full of glittering women and their tolerantly smiling men, who, though giving the impression that they had been dragged there reluctantly, seemed reasonably disposed to enjoy themselves. If only Guy would seem half as indulgent Celia would not have felt in such a dither. Which in London was a word she had been taught to forget she had ever known.

But if Celia was to feel utterly demoralised inside, it certainly did not show. She was beautiful and moved like a dream, her slender, graceful body as lissom as a dancer's. She looked young, much younger than her twenty-three years, and her skin had a breathtaking purity, a creamy paleness which deepened at times to an almond blossom flush. Across the stage, on the few occasions she appeared, she seemed to float, to be imbued with some transparently ethereal quality impossible to pin down. The audience was entirely charmed, the applause at the end of each short appearance entirely spontaneous. It was something of a novelty to find so lovely a girl so obviously gifted. Even the way in which she compered the show, as she described each dress, was something to be admired. That she was clearly responsible for the success of the evening was very apparent to everyone there. Guy Ryland was indeed fortunate to have her.

'Didn't you hear them whispering?' Guy mocked much later, as he personally carried over to her a drink as she tried to wedge unseen into a secluded corner, an alcove in the large living-room of his town flat. Immediately she regretted such a manoeuvre, which isolated them from the mainstream of the crowd, but when she glanced rather

151

furtively around for a means of escape he merely placed his hand to the wall, blocking all hopes of successfully achieving it.

'Don't you want to hear my congratulations?' he drawled deliberately blind to her obvious panic.

Celia clutched her drink too tightly, turning her eyes helplessly to its sparkling depth and, trying not to remember another occasion when she had been pinned against a wall. 'One gets a little weary,' she feigned sophisticated indifference, lifting her shoulders almost imperceptibly. 'I can't think anything's been left unsaid.'

'Nothing, you mean, you want to listen to from me?'

'Naturally,' she murmured, with some abstraction, 'you being the boss and all that ...'

'Naturally,' he repeated, his eyes narrowed dangerously but his voice softer than she had heard it in a long time, and the hand he laid suddenly on her shoulder was gentle. Celia didn't know he could see how her own hand trembled, nor that the sudden draining of nervous energy reflected tensely in the whiteness of her face. His hand slid to her nape which her thin chiffon dress left bare, his lean fingers caressing her skin, easing the tension from her.

'Better?' His eyes, insistent, drew hers, and reading in their clouded blueness a certain degree of surrender, his own gleamed with restrained satisfaction.

'If better is loving you to distraction!' Almost Celia spoke the words aloud and, horrified, drew back, the implication of such thoughts a catastrophe, the possibility of uttering them so that he might hear a disaster! 'You have other guests,' she said, her voice jerking, the force of self-revelation almost spinning her on her feet. Faintly she heard herself continuing, 'You can't neglect them.'

He didn't deny or confirm it, he merely smiled slightly, his attention still with her. 'After this lot has departed I'll take you home.'

'I'll get Robin——'

Never, she vowed, could she risk being alone with him

again. She ought not to have come here this evening. She hadn't intended to, but Guy had collected her as the last dress had been auctioned to a triumphant bidder, making it impossible for her to slip away unnoticed as she had planned. Fortunately his car, coming here, had been crammed with other members of the staff and she had sat as far away from him as she could manage. 'Robin will do nicely,' she reaffirmed, with a vaguely happier smile.

Guy's smile was fractionally tighter than her own, as if he had her measure and made sure he was one step ahead. 'Robin's gone already. He has, I believe, an assignation at the other side of town.'

'Which you encouraged!'

'Not necessarily. He'd done his duty here. There was no point in holding him any longer.'

Fretfully she moved her head. 'Robin has various girl-friends, I suppose, but neither Lucy or I are allowed to meet them.'

'You will—when he begins to take one seriously.'

'I wonder if he ever will?'

Guy's tone was dryer. 'Most men don't care for chains, Celia, not if they can avoid them.'

'And that's the way you look at marriage!'

'One tries to avoid such a commitment,' he agreed.

'Until you find someone who qualifies on every point. You sound as if you consider it in the same light as engaging a secretary, Mr Ryland.'

'Oh, not quite,' his mouth quirked. 'I should definitely prefer one able to cook a little. Later, Celia, when we have the place to ourselves, you might like to try your hand at an omelette. I don't remember eating much all day, and we have things to talk over.'

Filled with a growing confusion, Celia subsided, still clinging to her remote corner, her half-empty glass of champagne becoming flat in her hand, as motionless as she felt herself. What had he meant when he'd mentioned having things to talk over? Had the bit about the omelette been merely incidental, a vague idea pushed into the conversation by a momentary twinge of hunger, or had it been deliberate, and consequently something to worry about? How was she to know? The involvement of her emotions was something she had never bargained for, not with Guy Ryland, and her only conscious reaction was one of fright. There was also an instinctive urge to retreat, like some small creature in the wilds when faced with a predator much larger in every way than itself.

The knowledge that she loved Guy had caught her unawares, giving her no chance to organize any sort of defence against it. It was as unexplainable as it was illogical, as long ago she had wholeheartedly settled for hating him. For years she had longed to meet someone special, one particular man, whom she might love to distraction; surely then it proved a cruel twist of fate that this man should turn out to be Guy Ryland!

If Celia had hoped to make a quiet getaway she was doomed to disappointment. While he circulated among his other guests Guy also managed to keep a watchful eye on her every move, outmanoeuvring her at every turn. Without making another scene there was nothing she could do but wait, outwardly compliant but finding even the pretence of enjoying herself an almost intolerable strain. She hated Guy's obvious imperviousness in such direct contrast to her own inner turmoil, and she knew she would be in no fit condition to resist him if he should demand again that she apologised. This, she was convinced, was what he wanted to talk about—after the others had gone!

The show had exhausted her, leaving her unnaturally pale, and beneath a superficial gaiety there still remained a current of tension. She was only half aware of people beginning to leave, of farewells being said before the final exodus of the majority. Once they were left on their own, the flat, which took up the entire top floor of a large old house at the end of a suburban road, seemed too silent, much too empty.

'It's too big for me really,' Guy shrugged after the last departing guest. 'For years I've considered getting rid of it, but it has its uses, especially for entertaining on occasions like this.'

Celia made no immediate comment, feeling in that instance, as he stood contemplating her, utterly beyond one. She had not properly considered how it would be like to be so alone with a man who could make her pulses race merely by looking at her. She had been foolish not to have left early. There must have been some opportunity. Guy must know for certain that there had been, and would no doubt be congratulating himself that she hadn't taken it.

'I'm quite ready to go now,' she said, her voice, although she didn't intend it to be, pleading.

'What about my omelette?' Swiftly he deterred her swift movement to pick up her wrap.

'It's too late.' Her words were a scarcely articulate sound of protest as he grasped her wrist, his fingers holding relentlessly the fine bone, sending a blaze of fire over her skin.

'Celia!' His voice edged with some amusement, he laughed. 'It's barely eleven. You'll be telling me next it's long past your bedtime.'

'Well, even so, you can't expect me to slave over a hot stove ...'

'No, of course not. You're quite right,' he regarded her for a moment with mock seriousness. 'You've probably had a harder day than I have. I'll cook my own supper, and yours. It's surprising how empty cocktail snacks can leave one.'

Celia glanced at him quickly. Was he speaking generally? She didn't remember seeing him eat one thing the whole evening. Suddenly she had the barely creditable feeling that, for some reason or another, her was merely using small-talk, something Lucy occasionally indulged in when she wanted to cover up. With a thin shiver of unexplainable apprehension her mind was diverted.

155

'Lucy . . .?' Unwittingly Celia spoke aloud.

'Yes.' His eyebrows raised, Guy looked down at her vaguely anxious face, and when she made no immediate reply, he added quietly, 'You told me she'd gone out.'

'Yes. Yes, of course.'

Guy's mouth compressed ever so slightly. 'Then why the apparent concern? Where has she gone?'

Not caring for the rapid sequence of questions, his returning air of intolerance, Celia blinked, her long lashes falling over wary eyes. 'I'm not sure . . .'

'Has she gone with Denis?'

'I'm not sure. Probably,' she replied indistinctly, well aware that her evasive mumbling was annoying the man beside her, but too steeped in family loyalty to find it easy to discuss her sister's affairs with someone who so frankly disapproved of her. Swiftly, seeking a diversion, she used the only one she thought might do. 'If you like,' she said, attempting a light smile, 'I'll stay and cook your supper— if you show me where the kitchen is?'

'Is it a bargain?' he asked, leading the way.

'I don't know what you mean,' she shrugged vaguely, knowing quite well what he was talking about.

The kitchen, though beautifully fitted with every conceivable gadget, was small, scarcely large enough to accommodate two people. In the confined space Celia was too conscious of Guy's nearness and found it increasingly difficult to concentrate on what she was doing. She hoped her relief didn't show on her face when he suggested they carried their meal on trays to his study, the lounge still being covered with a litter of empty glasses which she considered doubtfully ought to have been washed and put away.

'My Mrs Mopp will clear it in the morning.' Guy followed her faintly unhappy gaze with indifferent eyes as he firmly closed the study door. 'I never let anyone in here.'

'I expect you usually eat out?' The study was reasonably spacious, and her omelettes a success, and Celia began to feel more relaxed.

'Quite often.' They shared a small table in front of the glowing electric fire and he looked at her across the shining top of it. 'But only because I don't prefer to eat alone.'

Strange how it seemed absolutely necessary to keep talking, to pursue some trivial conversation. Taking a quick, barely elegant gulp of the wine he poured her, she said, 'How do you like being a shopkeeper, as opposed to manufacturing, I mean?'

His smile was lazy, as if he was willing to humour her, at least for a while. 'I don't really care for shopkeeping, as you call it, at all, but it does provide one answer to an ever-increasing problem. Fate decrees we must do many things today, should we hope to survive, and I believe that our good Lord still helps those who are willing to help themselves.'

What a strange thing for him to say! Celia laid her fork down uncertainly.

'My ancestors, Celia, were mill owners in what I suppose are commonly known as the bad old days, so I expect manufacturing is somewhat steeped in my blood.'

'But you don't think they really were bad old days?' She knew a compulsion to challenge him, to sneer at his cast-iron imperviousness.

'Certainly they were bad at times, but inevitably so. It hasn't seemed possible to span the centuries anywhere without some measure of cruelty and exploitation of the people. To some extent it's still going on in parts of the world in this the twentieth century. And it's little use feeling superior, Celia. We probably wouldn't have acted any differently ourselves should we have been born into that particular era.'

'I wonder?' She knew he was aware of her desire to upset him, just as she realised how ineffective were any methods she might use against strength such as his. The best she could manage was to let him see she was quite unimpressed. 'I still believe men were too greedy—some still are today.'

'Perhaps,' he grinned. 'When it comes to something they

really want they can be ruthless as well.'

She hadn't been prepared for the dry amusement in his voice, nor the subtle implication in what he said, and while she flushed hotly his next words seemed to confound her discomfiture.

'There was a time, Celia, when Manchester was the centre of a new civilisation. It was here, in the nineteenth century, that the Industrial Revolution was invented. Coal produced steam, providing a far greater power than had ever been known, but it drove men as well. Things invariably get worse before they get better, and things did gradually begin to improve.'

'Over the last decade,' she agreed reluctantly.

'But for the cotton industry,' he countered, 'it hasn't been so good. After the First World War the markets which Lancashire relied on were lost. Among others, Japan with her advanced machinery took Lancashire's place, and in the 1920s the boom broke for ever. Since then it's been a struggle to keep going, but those earlier years were nothing to what it is now. If my great-grandfather could come back from the grave he would jump straight back into it again if faced with even a fraction of the problems we have to cope with today.'

'Really ...' His frankness faintly scandalised, and she still wasn't sure whose side he was on. His clipped, sardonic tones had merely indicated a desire to straighten her out with a few facts, without the need to bore. She had the feeling that with a little encouragement he could go on and on—that the history of Manchester and its people was something very near to his heart, something he seldom got tired of talking or hearing about. And above all he loved his factories, devoting far more time and energy to them than ever he expended on his shops.

Celia sighed as she pushed away her tray. 'Mill owners, it's been said, used to take their pick of the women workers.'

He laughed, his teeth gleaming white. 'Well, my grandfather certainly wouldn't enjoy that privilege today.'

Mortified, she stared down at her clenched hands. What on earth had made her say such a thing? 'I'm sorry,' she murmured, unable to analyse her own feelings. Suddenly horrified, she felt almost ready to weep, the degree of her heightened emotions swinging like a pendulum against her.

Guy, with one swift, narrowed glance, pushed the table to one side, coming lithely to his feet, and bent down to bring her gently up to him. 'What is it?' he asked in a low voice, his hands gripping her bare arms as he drew her softly towards him.

'Nothing.' She shook her shining head, resisting him, yet making no protest when he ran exploratory fingers through her heavy, tumbled hair, so that her hot forehead pressed against him. 'I think I must be tired,' she breathed, her voice muffled and sounding strange, even to her own ears.

From the gentleness of his fingers she might have expected some words of comfort, but he only said slowly, 'You might feel better if you could bring yourself to utter the apology you owe me, instead of suggesting I might enjoy illicit relationships with too many of my female employees.'

How could she speak when her heart beat so rapidly? Restraint held her taut. She dared not let go or he might guess something of what she felt for him. She achieved a small helpless shrug, knowing well she was being whirled into danger. 'I'm sorry, Guy,' she whispered, suddenly taking the only way out, knowing she could expect nothing from him unless she was prepared to give a little, but with feminine perversity unable to stop herself adding, 'Didn't this evening make up for some of my failures in other directions?'

One heavy eyebrow rose. 'You can't be unaware that I've left the damned wall where it is. It's taken a bit of sorting out—that, and my temper!'

Weakly she said, 'Because of the additional expense, I suppose?'

159

'Expense!' he repeated, almost savagely. 'If I felt so inclined I could knock Kingsley's down and rebuild it again, and never count the cost!'

'And you think money can buy you anything!' Irrationally hurt by his tone, she tried to pull away, only to find herself held tighter.

'Celia,' his eyes glittered, 'can't you ever get rid of that chip on your shoulder?'

'It's not a chip, as you so crudely call it. You said some rather horrible things,' her voice choked, 'I've had a miserable week, and now you tell me that expense didn't—doesn't matter!'

'Were you miserable because of how I spoke to you, or because of the things I said?'

'Because of the way you . . .' Aghast, Celia's voice trailed off. Almost he had wrung from her a confession she would rather not think about. 'Please take me home,' she begged, the back of her fingers taut against her lips to stop them trembling.

It didn't help that there was in his expression an almost diabolical gleam of satisfaction, and he made no immediate move to comply with her wishes. 'You don't have to fight me all the way, you know. It might even be to your advantage to unbend a little. You're too lovely to be lonely.'

If only he would take his arms away she might be able to think straight. 'Because I haven't a boy-friend, I suppose you mean?' She was well aware that since returning to the store she had committed the same folly as before by throwing herself wholeheartedly into her work to the exclusion of everything else. The once or twice she had been asked out she had refused; to begin with because she had begrudged the time, but now, feeling as she did about Guy, because there wouldn't be much point. Carefully she added, 'A boy-friend is something I shelved until I re-established myself.'

Again his smile glinted coolly, 'Why bother? You'd only

be wasting their time and your own. I don't want you going out with anyone, Celia.'

Small shivers of alarm drifted through her. 'I don't understand. My free time is my own.'

He watched her narrowly. 'I think you understand as well as I do, Celia. I believe we have something between us. Nothing you might feel that's very tangible, but until we get it out of our systems you could do well to leave other men alone.'

'Why ...' She lifted her head in a shock of protest, conscious suddenly of the lateness of the hour and that very thing between them which she had been about to deny but was unable to ignore.

Guy stared at her as the words died in her throat, at her slender, chiffon-clad figure which was all allure. When she stirred there was the faint scent of some musky perfume from the seductive hollow at the low neckline of her dress. 'You could almost drive a man mad,' he said, not mocking any more but with a hard line of restraint around his mouth as he found her lips.

As he kissed her, Celia found herself melting against him, held by the spell of her own excitement and of the way he held her, the new look in his eyes, the deeper note in his voice. Her heart was beating fast, her mind whirling in heady delight. He had kissed her before, it seemed many times, but this was different, completely different because she loved him, and the knowledge brought with it a rapture she didn't attempt to deny. Her arms went up around his neck and she closed her eyes, letting his kisses take her very being as they scorched her trembling mouth.

When he raised his head he heard her caught breath as defensively she buried her hot face against his shoulder. When he put his fingers beneath her chin and forced her to look at him her eyes were soft and deep, in the dim light a little starry, and her lips the lips of a woman pleading to be kissed. He heard her little cry of desperation as almost brutally he brought her to him again, her silent plea for

161

mercy something to be ignored. And after a moment she returned his kisses, not caring what he read into the tumult of her response.

Then he let her go, quite abruptly, a kind of caution playing in his eyes as they swept over her. 'I'll take you home now,' was all he said.

Celia heard herself making a curious little sound, a half sob which drowned her low, half-hysterical exclamation. She was swaying, giddy, her head drooping so that she could scarcely see. She had been whirling intensely through time into space and the sudden transition back to reality left her wholly unbalanced.

'Come on,' he commanded, his dark eyes lingering on her full, quivering mouth. 'Where's the girl who's always so cool!'

Cool! Anger and humiliation exploded in her head as she wrenched away from him and groped for her wrap. She had wanted so much to stay, his arms were becoming in some way very necessary to her, yet each time he held her he seemed to take a perverse pleasure in rejecting her. Or did he intend, she wondered bleakly, to bring her to such a pitch as to make the last hurdle completely assailable—when he chose?

It seemed she was right when his hand on her arm stayed her a moment. 'There are some things you have to be sure about, Celia, and I don't think this evening you're in any fit state to make the kind of decisions which would please you in the morning.'

Did he always have to be so condescending? she wondered bleakly, as some time later she let herself into the silent house in Moorland Road. How utterly fortunate he was to be able to switch from one phase to another without notable effort. How expertly had he dealt with her youth and inexperience, restricting her with what could only be termed as skilled proficiency to one step at a time!

He had brought her home, handing her into his car as if she was suddenly infinitely precious, which, Celia con-

162

cluded bitterly, might all be a calculated art. Yet he had held her hand for the greater part of the way, his thumb caressing on her soft palm until her own fingers had curled around his tightly, unable to withstand a renewed surge of pleasure.

'Am I to be forgiven?' he had asked in a low voice as they parted, and had seemed entirely satisfied with the slow, if uncomprehending, lift of her head.

Forgiven? As she stayed momentarily with her back against the closed door listening to his receding footsteps, the sound of his engine restarting and softly revving, she pondered dreamily on his last words. She had nodded but hadn't really known what he had meant. It could be many things, but whatever it was she knew she would be prepared to forgive him most anything now. She seemed to have few defences left against him. All her former antagonism, all her previous hate appeared to have been swept away before the open floodgates of this new love she had for him. It was as if her old dislike of him has never existed, or had merely served as a disguise for these stronger feelings which threatened to sweep her off her feet and to bear her ruthlessly forward into a situation from which she might not easily be able to extricate herself.

Moving rather blindly, Celia caught sight of Lucy's coat flung carelessly over a chair in the hall and knew a flicker of relief that the girl was in. She opened her bedroom door, but could only discern the uneven contours of the bed and closed the door again softly. Lucy didn't like being disturbed once she was asleep, and, this evening, wanting only to be alone with her own thoughts, Celia had no desire to disturb her. In spite of being so tired she was still awake when she heard Robin come in, and it was only after that that she fell into an uneasy sleep, her heightened emotions giving way at last before the all-prevailing exhaustion of her body.

Naturally it was later than usual next morning when she awoke. For one wonderful moment she lay, unconsciously relaxed, wrapped in a kind of warm cocoon of unreality, and allowed her mind to be wholly preoccupied with a flicker of light from the window. It came through a slight gap in the curtains, making small, shifting mosaic patterns on the wall. It was then that she caught sight of the time and, filled with dismay, she almost fell out of bed. Guy had said not to hurry in, but if she didn't make an effort Lucy and Robin would be late, as they didn't seem able to get up without her.

Down in the kitchen she tried to restore some semblance of order. Because of the dress show she hadn't managed to return home the evening before, and felt ashamed to see the previous morning's dishes still in the sink. Lucy had promised to do them.

'She must have forgotten,' Robin quoted the obvious with bleary-eyed indifference, excusing his younger sister as usual. It was like some sort of conspiracy, Celia fretted, and she supposed Robin wasn't entirely to blame. He had become so used to keeping an eye on Lucy that he seemed to consider her more in the light of a tolerant parent, and didn't seem to mind that the girl very rarely did a hand's turn, but left it all to Celia.

'You might pop upstairs and see what she's doing,' Celia retorted, restraining a sharper retort as she juggled with the coffee pot and toaster. 'I did knock on her door as I passed, but she can't have heard.' With a rueful sigh she plugged in the percolator. For no reason at all this morning, she felt overwrought as well as tired.

Reluctantly Robin did as she requested, but two minutes later he was back in the kitchen, his usual complacency obviously disturbed. 'She isn't there,' he said, 'nor does her bed appear to have been slept in!'

'Not slept in?' Celia stared at him, a terrible fear gripping the lower part of her stomach. 'You surely can't mean she's gone?'

'There might,' Robin frowned, coming to the table as he

ran perplexed fingers through his unruly hair, 'be some quite simple explanation.'

Couldn't he think of anything better than the standard comment? 'Robin!' Celia's face was suddenly very pale. 'You don't think she's stayed out overnight with Denis?'

'No good heavens, surely not!' Celia watched her brother shrink beneath a dawning consternation.

'Has she ever,' Celia asked steadily, trying to take a grip of herself, 'stayed out before?'

'No, never. Well, not anywhere I haven't known about. She's inclined to be headstrong, like you, but that isn't to say she's foolhardy.'

Celia glanced at him swiftly as she distractedly switched off the percolator, not liking the allusion to her own failings. It was no comfort that Guy had said much the same thing, and the comparison hurt. But this wasn't the time to dwell on herself! Robin clearly wasn't at his best in an emergency. 'I'll just take one more look upstairs,' she said quickly, 'you could have missed her.'

While knowing instinctively that it was futile from the very beginning, Celia searched, but of course there was no sign of the missing Lucy. There was just her coat, still over the chair where Celia had seen it as she came in the evening before, 'It's the one she's been wearing lately,' she told an agitated Robin as she ran down again. 'When I saw it I immediately assumed she was in, and when I looked into her bedroom I thought she was in bed. I see now it was simply the untidy blankets.'

'I'd better give Denis a ring.' Robin got heavily to his feet, as if the gravity of the situation had just hit him. 'When I get hold of the little so-and-so I'll wring her neck!'

'Robin, wait!' Celia reached him at the telephone, her hand on the receiver. 'What if she isn't—wasn't with Denis? There really might, as you said, be a very simple explanation, but the whole situation could be misconstrued. If she wasn't with Denis and he learns she hasn't been here all night . . . oh, don't you see?' she cried, as Robin looked irritatingly blank, 'she might be anywhere and I know how fond she is of Denis. I wouldn't want to do anything to spoil her chances.'

'But where else could she be?'

'I don't know—but you know as well as I do that rumours, particularly nasty ones, can start so easily. It's possible she could have stayed with a girl friend. Goodness knows, she seems to have plenty.'

'And you think she could have gone straight on to work? She would have given us a ring, surely!'

'You know Lucy.'

Robin's face held a bewildered expression. 'You're suggesting we see if she's at the shop before doing anything else?'

Celia bit her lip until it hurt. 'Half an hour can't make much difference,' she said, desperately praying she was right, trying to remain calm, if only for Robin's sake. 'It could be important to her—I mean, the way we handle this.'

All the way to the shop Celia worried. Why hadn't she made doubly sure Lucy was in when she herself had come home? Was she crazy not to have rung the police straight away, to have stopped Robin ringing Denis? Lucy might have had an accident, or been murdered—attacked. Wasn't it happening every day? Only one never thought, somehow, of it happening to oneself, or to anyone one knew.

Robin checked immediately they arrived to see if Lucy was at the shop, but it seemed she was not. She wasn't in the office and no one had seen her. 'I know it sounds uncaring,' he added, with an air of some harassment, 'but I must just show my face at my end before I do anything more. Guy has been far from easy lately and I'd better not make things worse. If I were you, Celia, I'd give Denis a ring now. And from your office, where you haven't a secretary popping in and out. We don't want to cause another stir like the last one, or we'll have Guy raising the roof again. When you've got hold of Denis let me know. I'll wait until I hear from you.'

Her temper on edge in spite of her anxiety, Celia stared after him. She knew he referred to the unfortunate incident of the alterations, and wondered resentfully why, when he must know how worried she was about Lucy, he had bothered to mention it at all. It was like the rubbing of salt into a still raw wound, making her doubt unhappily her newly patched up relationship with Guy.

In her office she closed the door firmly and rang through to Denis. He must have arrived by now. How did one ask a man if one's sister had spent the night with him? It was only now that she realised why Robin had been evasive. He must have been asking himself the same thing. As the line purred she pondered. Inspiration might come, but it couldn't completely save the situation, as Robin must have known only too well.

To her dismay Denis was not in, nor, when she rang his flat, was he there either, and she spent the next ten minutes ringing alternately his home and office without any success. Eventually, not knowing what else to do, she left word with one of the typists that he should contact her immediately he arrived. Which seemed all she could do in that direction, she tried to assure herself, for the time being.

But it wasn't terribly satisfactory, and she was still sitting staring at the telephone when it rang, at that moment so startlingly unexpected that visibly she jumped. Her nerves taut, she picked up the receiver. Would Celia come at once to Mr Ryland's office? Mr Guy Ryland?

With some uneasiness Celia hedged. 'Is it urgent?' she asked, knowing a curious reluctance to see Guy before this business about Lucy was cleared up. He didn't care for Lucy, and she didn't want to be forced to confess what had happened. Somehow, after being in his arms so recently she felt his cynicism would be more than she could possibly bear. As his secretary pondered, Celia waited.

There was a short silence, then Guy came on the line himself. His voice was terse to the point of being angry. 'Celia, I want you up here right away,' he said. 'Don't argue!'

CHAPTER TEN

ONCE again Celia found herself staring at the replaced receiver as Guy abruptly hung up. His voice had been curt, unmistakably so, and even across the line she had sensed a measure of coldness, almost as if their closeness the evening before had never existed. It seemed like a bad omen, which of course was surely ridiculous, except, Celia reminded herself sharply, in the present circumstances. It might just be possible that already Guy might know something about Denis and Lucy, something to justify the present state of his temper. Fright whirling through her, Celia hesitated no longer, and with her mind clogged with apprehension she didn't even remember Robin would be waiting.

Guy's face, as she had feared, was uncompromising. He was standing beside the window, looking out over the conglomeration of rain-soaked rooftops which glinted fitfully where a transient sun caught the dark grey slate. He gave the impression, although she could scarcely believe it of Guy Ryland, of a man who had been pacing uneasily up and down.

He turned immediately Celia entered, and, to her utter confusion he walked over to where she stood and dropped a brief kiss on her nervous lips, his hand beneath her chin. From the corner of her eye she seemed to see his secretary's almost visible start of surprise as she closed the door.

'You shouldn't have done that,' she said blankly.

'Perhaps not,' he agreed enigmatically, slowly releasing her and pulling out a chair so she might sit down. 'You might do better with a drink.'

'A drink?' Somehow his words·had an ominous ring. 'Why should you think I would need one particularly?'

'Celia——' he remained looking down at her for another short moment before going back to his own chair behind his desk: intentionally or not, something about his eyes frightened her. 'I received a letter, or rather a note, this morning,' he went on, 'from Denis. There's little point in beating about the bush. In it he tells me he's getting married, and, as he has some holiday due, he hopes I won't mind. He goes on to say he may or may not be back. Most probably not. Here . . . there's more about a special licence and such, you'd better read it for yourself.'

With numb fingers reflecting her state of mind, Celia grasped the proffered note, suddenly not daring to look at him and glad of an excuse not to do so as her eyes clung to the brief message scribbled carelessly on an old piece of notepaper.

'It's not even clean,' she heard herself murmuring irrelevantly, stunned by the shock of Denis's disclosure while groping with the full implications. So this was where Lucy had gone! Hurt washed right through her that her sister could have gone off like this. Denis didn't actually mention her name, but it was an obvious omission. 'My future wife,' he wrote, 'has everything I've ever wished for—and I know you already like her.'

'Lucy!' Celia's voice rose on a thread of hysteria as she glanced resentfully at Guy. 'How wrong can you get?' she cried wildly. 'He must know very well you don't like her!'

She stared down at the scrap of paper again, fighting an incredulous disbelief, a losing battle for control, unaware of Guy's tightening lips, his quick frown. 'So it is Lucy,' he said. 'She isn't with you?'

She didn't understand the faint doubt in his expression. 'Lucy has been gone all night.' It seemed pointless now to

169

deny it. And what would be the use? It was, at least, something to know she was all right. But balanced against the comforting knowledge that she hadn't met with an accident, was the probably more horrifying awareness that she had been driven to this.

Dislike bleak in her eyes, she accused the man in front of her. 'You drove them to it, didn't you? You never approved of Lucy, and Denis was completely under your thumb. You would never have agreed to their marriage had they stayed here, and they knew it apparently only too well.'

'Celia!' His voice was harsh, and his mouth, the same mouth which had touched hers only a few minutes ago was set in hard lines. 'Don't you think it's time you came to your senses? I had nothing personally against your sister.'

'Why ...' In the throes of reaction, a white-hot fury gripped Celia forcibly, jerking her to her feet. Head flung back, she glared at him, words tripping off the end of her tongue with reckless disregard for any kind of caution. 'I never thought of you as a liar! You never had a good word to say for her. Or more accurately, any sort of word at all. You simply refused to talk about her.'

'Celia!'

But she swept on regardless of his warning tone. 'She was just never good enough for a Ryland, was she? And to think that but for your hate she could have been married here and had the sort of home she wanted, near those who loved her!'

'Will you shut up!' Guy was beside her now, gripping her shoulders, looking, as he had done before, as if he would enjoy shaking the life out of her. Only this time there was more. There was in his eyes a cold anger, a contemptuous dislike which might have frightened her had she been able to see it.

Celia, at that moment, could see nothing through the fine mist of rage that blinded her vision. She could only feel his fingers biting into her skin through the thin material of her dress, and was revolted that the familiar thrill of fire should go through her at his touch. Surely now she should be immune? Wildly she struggled. 'Let me go!' she positively screamed, the hysteria in her voice unmistakable.

Without hesitation Guy Ryland lifted his hand and slapped her lightly across one cheek. 'I'm sorry,' he said, his eyes belying it, a muscle jerking at the side of his well disciplined mouth, 'but you have to see reason.'

'I hate you—hate you!' she cried, quite beyond any sort of reason at all, tears streaming down cheeks still smarting from contact with his hand. 'I think I shall for the rest of my life!'

'Fine, then,' he jeered, 'you do that if it's going to make you feel any better.' His face set coldly and Celia felt he was a stranger, but she was trembling so hard that it scarcely registered. She was barely aware that he put a drink into her hands and forced her to swallow it. 'That,' he said tonelessly, 'is just to stop you making a complete fool of yourself.'

His words hit and hurt, yet they succeeded in pulling her up sharply. She went quiet as the office stopped spinning strangely. In another minute, she thought, measuring the space between herself and the door, I'll be able to get up and walk out. Her mind was still hazy and she felt ill, knowing that she had said too much. She had a vague feeling somewhere at the back of her mind that the old antagonism, which she had believed gone, had been behind a lot of the probably unforgivable things she had just uttered.

Attacking Guy, she realised dully, couldn't really help Lucy at all, especially if Denis and she were to return. And even if Guy had been indirectly responsible, Denis and Lucy were scarcely children. Surely, if they loved each other, they could have weathered any kind of storm, certainly any obstacle that Guy could put in their way? If they had wanted to live elsewhere they could quite easily have been married here in Manchester and then gone, without acting in such a melodramatic and totally disturbing fashion. With painful uncertainty she stared at her fingers without seeing them, feeling instinctively that she had made a terrible mistake. How could she pretend to love Guy if she neither liked or trusted him?

He had turned and walked again to the window where he stood unconsciously tapping the narrow window ledge, seemingly deep in thought, and Celia gazed at the back of his dark head, her heart full of painful regret. 'Guy,' she whispered, seeing suddenly, with clarity, the impression her words and actions must have given. If he had slapped her he had had good reason, and she must admit it and apologise, then go and consult Robin, who would be waiting. 'Guy ...' she repeated, as he did not seem to have heard her, but she doubted if he did this time either, as the telephone rang in the middle of her agonised little murmur.

Swiftly he pounced, picking it up, his movements so like a man nearing the end of a limited patience that Celia caught her breath. 'Yes?' he exclaimed, his voice clipped.

Celia, desperately trying to pull herself together, didn't really listen. Nor did she look, or she might have been puzzled by his change of expression as he finished speaking and stood regarding her, a quick frown on his face. He wore the expression of a man approaching a particularly hazardous crossing on a relatively unknown road.

'I don't know how you're going to take this, Celia,' he said. 'That happened to be Greta Morrison's father, and she, apparently, is the girl whom Denis has eloped with.'

'Greta!' After the first exclamation of startled dismay Celia gazed at him wordlessly. It hadn't been Lucy after all! Lucy must still be here! But the surge of positive relief was immediately drowned by the recollection of her own behaviour, and another aspect which was even more frightening, 'I feel sorry for the Morrisons,' she said stiffly, 'but where can Lucy be?'

'Perhaps she's at home after all?' Guy suggested dryly.

'No! That is, she couldn't be.' This new aspect, coming as it did on top of what had gone before, caught Celia unawares. She ought to be commiserating about Greta or

Denis, or maybe both, as the news of their going must have shocked Guy, but all she could think of was Lucy. 'I have a feeling,' she cried, 'something dreadful has happened. I've felt it all along. I must go and find Robin.'

'Have you forgotten you both work here?'

'Oh ...' Her face scarlet, Celia halted in her tracks. But perhaps, she reminded herself, she was in need of some rebuke. 'Guy,' she began painfully, 'I'm sorry. I promised Robin I would let him know as soon as I knew anything. You can't really want to help, not after ...'

'Sit down again, Celia!' His voice was presumptuous and he ignored her stumbling hesitations, as if her attempted apology was of no interest whatsoever. 'Lucy could be at home in spite of what you say. If not we'll soon find her. After that I'll go and see the Morrisons. I can only hope they won't have as much to say as you.'

'Why should they?' Celia asked between trembling lips as she almost collapsed into her seat, for once almost glad to do as she was told. She watched uncertainly as he began dialling, his stony gaze fixed in a detached fashion on her white, shaken face. 'Why should they?' she insisted stubbornly.

'Because,' he exclaimed, as the number purred, 'Greta is an only child, as well as being a considerable heiress, and they had, I gather, great plans for her which didn't include Denis.'

'Who are you ringing?' She had known Greta's parents were wealthy, but surely Greta had been in love with Guy? And she had believed that Guy had either wanted Greta himself, or planned to marry her, as Robin had said, to Denis.

'I've been ringing your home, but Lucy is obviously not there.'

'But I told you—we looked all over, and we couldn't have missed her.'

'I'll try the office, and if she hasn't turned up the only logical alternative is the police.' His voice was cold, perfectly controlled, a polite stranger. 'She could have had an accident.'

'Surely not! I did think about it, but Robin ...'

'It's a possibility.'

At that moment the telephone rang again. It was Guy's secretary with a message. 'The hospital called, sir. Miss Kingsley was admitted last night after a slight accident. She would like to speak to her sister.'

'Thank you.' Guy replaced the receiver, frowning, but not attempting to hide from Celia what could only be bad news. 'That was about Lucy,' he enlightened her immediately. 'She's in hospital but not badly hurt, or so I believe.'

Celia felt herself go cold with shock. This was something she hadn't wanted to contemplate although she had known Guy was speaking the truth when he had said it was a possibility. 'What happened?' she managed to get out as she stumbled to her feet, a wave of fear running right through her.

'They aren't sure yet.' Warily his eyes were on her distraught face, and seeing her sway visibly he was around at her side, his hand beneath her arm holding her firmly. 'Apparently she was only concussed, which might not be very serious but which would explain why she couldn't let you know. Of course my secretary only took a message.'

'I must go,' Celia heard herself saying. Guy's hand was impersonal, but she was grateful for it's steadying influence. 'I must tell Robin first, of course.'

'I'll give him a ring while you collect a coat, or better still I'll send someone down for one. Then I'll take you to the hospital myself. If necessary Robin can come later.'

It didn't occur to Celia to argue. She waited numbly while Guy saw to all these things, then went with him to find Lucy. She would rather have gone with Robin, as she was well aware that Guy only accompanied her because it seemed the polite thing to do. He was remote and made no attempt to offer so much as a word of comfort after they left the shop. His hand warm beneath her arm might never

174

have been. They were back again, it seemed, on their old level of strained formality, the new relationship which had developed so compulsively between them gone for ever. Her mind swamped with shock and confusion, Celia was aware of this, and felt the swift pain of loss even while her thoughts were almost entirely absorbed with Lucy.

How could she have been wandering about by herself? It didn't make sense. She had been going to meet Denis after the dress show, and now it seemed he had gone off with another woman.

Greta Morrison! Unknowingly, Celia turned to stare at Guy blankly. Of course she had been friendly with Denis. Lucy had been aware that he had often taken Greta out, but none of them had ever been given reason to suspect they were in love. Greta had taken part in the show, and she had worked quite hard. Surely one couldn't do that and run away immediately afterwards to get married? And if Guy was in love with her what must he be feeling? For the hundredth time that morning Celia wondered why nothing seemed to add up.

Her heart aching with a peculiar kind of compassion, Celia continued to study him as he drove as swiftly through the crowded streets as he was able. He did have the appearance of a man withdrawn and cold, as if Greta's impending marriage had induced a hard, frozen indifference. And, Celia knew with a surge of shame, her own attitude couldn't have helped. She had tried once before to apologise, and he had indicated quite clearly that he wasn't prepared to listen, yet she couldn't stop herself at that moment from trying again.

'I'm sorry,' she said in a low voice, the hint of strain unmistakable, 'I shouldn't have spoken as I did.' She didn't ask his forgiveness, knowing from the arrogantly indifferent set of his jaw it would not be forthcoming, but if nothing else, the few words she had managed seemed to ease a little of her own painful tenseness.

175

'Forget it.' His lips went tight, and not even for a second did he turn his head.

The blood rushed to Celia's face and she caught her lip between her teeth, conscious that his short utterance was a mere formality and nothing else. There seemed nothing else to say and, quivering with a cold misery, she shrank back in her corner and kept her mind fixed determinedly on Lucy for the remainder of the way.

Once at the hospital she was quickly taken to her sister, and Guy stalked by her side, giving the impression, she thought bitterly, that she was something to be protected from any of the rougher issues which might emerge.

Lucy, to her surprise and relief, was awake and looking quite cheerful in spite of the bandages around her head. 'Hello, darling,' she cried, before Celia could speak. 'I expect you wondered where I'd got to?'

'Darling!' For one whole minute Celia was unable to speak. Her eyes filled with foolish tears and her soft lips trembled. 'It's so wonderful that you're safe,' she whispered, her relief at finding Lucy comparatively unharmed superseding all else. 'We've been so worried, Robin and I. When you weren't in your bed this morning we couldn't think what could have happened!'

'It was really the fault of my silly shoes,' Lucy began, not very explicitly, as Celia, mindful of her bandaged head, hugged her gently. 'I think I stumbled off the pavement almost in front of a bus.'

'It caught the side of your head,' Celia amended, having spoken with the ward Sister. 'You were concussed and must be quiet for a day or two, but otherwise you're all right.'

'You are also an extremely lucky girl,' Guy said wryly, coming up behind Celia.

'Guy!' Lucy glanced up too quickly and gave a little wince, but Celia saw quite clearly that she was flattered. 'How nice to see you, Guy. I'll have all the nurses asking who you are after you've gone.' Her eyes lingered appreciatively on his tall handsome figure. 'I realise I was

176

lucky,' she conceded, 'but it was ages this morning before I could remember exactly who I was. You see,' she glanced at Celia, 'I'd taken my new handbag and hadn't put in any form of identification. A handkerchief, I think, and some money, that was all. But of course as soon as I did remember I asked them to ring you.'

She didn't say anything about Denis and, as they had been specifically asked not to mention anything which might upset her, neither Celia nor Guy so much as spoke his name. After a few more minutes Guy said goodbye. Before he went he told Celia he would send a car back for her.

'Take the rest of the day off,' he said coldly, his eyes unfathomable on her pale face. 'You probably have things to fetch for Lucy, and after the show last night no doubt you must be tired.'

'Very magnanimous of him, surely,' Lucy exclaimed after he had gone, 'but he does look a bit grim—and I'm not flattering myself it's because of me. You haven't been quarrelling with him again, have you, darling?'

'No, not really.' Celia dived into Lucy's locker in order to avoid her brightly inquisitive glance. She could have confessed bleakly that quarrelling with Guy was fast becoming an almost permanent pastime!

Fortunately Lucy didn't seem to notice anything very much amiss. Celia, inspecting the empty cabinet with apparently absorbed concentration, heard her say idly, 'I sometimes wonder how Denis puts up with him.'

With an almost visible start Celia changed the conversation, but found to her dismay that Denis was not to be as easily dismissed as she supposed. Lucy's accident, in spite of her obvious desire to make light of it, had taken more out of her than she imagined, and her subsequent grumblings at having to stay in hospital soon faded into a more submissive murmur. As Celia rose to go, having been warned not to stay long this first time, Lucy asked if she would let Denis know where she was.

'I could give him a ring,' the girl added, 'but Sister won't hear of me using the telephone until I get a bit better.'

'What exactly did you want me to tell him?' Rather desperately Celia skirted around the truth, wishing to avoid harming Lucy in any possible way.

Lucy already had her eyes half closed and her voice sounded weary, yet she managed to reply. 'I didn't see him last night, you see. I was on my way to meet someone else when I collided with the bus; another man who was unable to come to the house and collect me. We were going on to a party.'

'Then you weren't with Denis!' Celia found herself exclaiming unnecessarily.

'We don't always go out together,' Lucy murmured sleepily, 'but I do like Denis a lot, and I know he likes me, so if you would just mention where I am I'd be grateful.'

'This other man,' Celia stared at her sister helplessly, 'won't he be wondering?'

'Oh, no. He'll just think I changed my mind, and he doesn't really matter. But as I've just told you, Denis is rather special.'

Celia took a deeply steadying breath. 'Do you really like him all that much?' It seemed a question she couldn't prevent herself from asking.

'Sometimes,' Lucy gave a little enigmatic laugh. 'But then I think he might go far. He has an eye for the main chance, that one, and it might pay me to stick around. I shouldn't mind being a Ryland wife, even with Guy controlling the purse strings. Think of all that money!'

Desperately Celia tried not to. It seemed incredible to her that Lucy's mind should work in such a fashion! Never before had she thought of her sister as mercenary and she wasn't at all sure she liked it.

As he had said he would, Guy sent his chauffeur back for her. He was waiting outside the hospital to take Celia home. For a fleeting moment she was tempted to defy such orders and return to the shop, but all of a sudden she felt deathly tired and weakly gave in. Even without Guy's permission to go straight home, she felt incapable of doing any other thing, and the shock of Lucy's accident on top of everything else became all at once, too much for her. Once in the house she sank down into a chair and promptly fell asleep, not even the dismal memory of Guy's last coldly cynical glance able to keep her awake.

It was almost dark before she aroused herself again, finding herself half frozen and chilled to the bone, and, apart from the physical aspects, she felt much worse than she could ever remember doing since she left London.

Next morning when she reached the shop she found to her dismay that Guy was gone, and when she asked his secretary she was merely told that Mr Ryland was out of town and it was not known when he might be expected back.

Robin, when consulted, confirmed that Guy was away for an indefinite period, and, although her heart ached painfully because of what she had heard, Celia felt angry, as she had on other occasions, by the smug satisfaction in Robin's voice. Already, she was aware, he was putting his mental feet up and would remain happily indolent until Guy returned. Did nothing ever shake him? she wondered as she reached her own domain. Not that Robin hadn't been upset about Lucy, he had, but he had got over it remarkably quickly when he realised she wasn't badly hurt.

A week later Celia was surprised to find a letter from Guy waiting for her at the shop. After days when the painful state of her emotions seemed almost more than she could bear, the sight of his hard masculine handwriting was like a personal touch, a gesture for which she craved, and as she stared down at the formal white envelope she felt herself almost blinded by tears.

Her heart fluttering in the old familiar way, she closed the door tightly, anxious to be quite alone. She had no idea what he could be writing to her about, but the fact that he had done so seemed to indicate that he had thought, even briefly, about her, and the knowledge was enough to make her pulses race.

'Celia,' he began, 'if you haven't already done so I should advise you to tell Lucy the truth. I have traced Denis and Greta—it wasn't particularly difficult, and they are well and truly married, and will shortly, I believe, be returning home. Greta's parents, it seems, have reluctantly given their blessing. At any rate they have agreed to take Denis into the firm which, you may or may not agree, is more than he deserves. Lucy, I think you'll find, won't be too surprised.

'As for myself, I expect to be away for several weeks, and as we can't have anything left to say to each other, you will probably be relieved. When I return I won't hold you to your contract any longer, and would recommend, if you feel so inclined, that you look for employment elsewhere. Guy Ryland.'

The letter came, with a touch of unforgiving anger, to an abrupt end, and Celia, entirely forgetting where she was, laid her head upon her desk and wept, the sobs of a suffocating despair shaking her slight body unmercifully.

The cruelty of his letter was like the sharp thrust of a knife. She had known he was angry, that he hadn't forgiven her, when he had gone away without a word, but she had never expected this. For years she had hated him, little suspecting that what she really felt was love, that this was the real reason why she had never been able to forget him. Why she had been drawn irrevocably back to Manchester before Christmas. Robin and Lucy had merely provided a means of evading the truth.

It seemed a long time before she found the strength to pull herself together, to raise her head and stare helplessly at the piece of damp crumpled paper in her hand which was all there was left of Guy's letter. It could be said he had wasted his time, as Lucy already knew about Greta and Denis. It had been impossible in the end to keep the news from her. Lucy had been startled, but Celia had been puzzled to find, as Guy had pointed out, not surprised.

After a few minutes of unhappy pondering Lucy had simply shrugged and wondered, as Celia had done, why Denis had found it necessary to run away.

'Greta will obviously inherit much more money than Denis will ever make, but I never thought he was in love with her,' was about all she had said.

Long before Celia reached home that evening she had made up her mind to go back to London. Aunt Mary was still in Torquay and looked like settling there permanently, but Celia didn't mind, having decided that a bed-sitter, or if she was lucky a small flat, would suit her better. She just couldn't contemplate returning to the old routine, to sit over a glowing fire of an evening while Aunt Mary knitted and dozed. After this, the kind of life she led mustn't allow time to think.

Lucy had been out of hospital several days and intended to start work again the following week. Neither she nor Robin raised any real objections when Celia told them of her plans to leave, and she realised somewhat bitterly that they would probably never miss her. Robin, although somewhat mystified that she should leave her very good job at the shop, had now got rid of his prevailing worry concerning Denis, and seemed quite content to let her go. Even so, Celia wouldn't have been happy about leaving them if she hadn't succeeded in finding a very good daily help. The lady was a youngish, middle-aged widow with time on her hands, who assured Celia that she would look after Robin and Lucy very well.

There only remained for her to say goodbye to Mrs Timpson, and as she was still extremely busy trying to get several things cleared up at the shop, Celia decided this could be done over the phone. Besides, to go to Guy's home was not to be considered at any cost. But Timmy, when she rang, almost begged her not to go without coming to see her at Cheverly.

'I would come to Manchester myself, dear,' she explained,

'but I haven't been well lately, and just couldn't face the journey even though it's not far.'

How could Celia refuse? If Timmy hadn't been ill she might have persuaded herself to do so, but it would seem heartless not to go now. She took the next afternoon off—she could make up the lost time the next day—and caught an early bus to Rossendale after lunch.

It was almost springtime, and after they left the city she saw the fields were already turning from the dull shades of winter to a fresher green. All around were unmistakable signs of nature returning to life even if the industrial landscape prevailed, and Celia thought nostalgically of how it would be further north in the wilder reaches of the Pennines, when at this time of the year there would be so much to see.

Her heart heavy, Celia stared from the bus window. She could, she supposed, have borrowed Robin's car, but she had been curiously disinclined to mention where she was going, as even to speak of anything remotely connected with Guy seemed to bring intolerable pain. Now, after feeling somewhat impatient with the slow progress of the bus, she felt a flicker of relief on reaching her destination. There had been other journeys in Guy's car which hadn't entailed a long walk from the village, but this she ignored.

Mrs Timpson was so delighted to see her that Celia felt in no small way compensated for all the heartache such a journey had caused her. 'You'll stay overnight, dear, won't you?' she was asked. 'You know Mr Guy wouldn't mind.'

'Oh, no, Timmy darling, I couldn't. I believe there's a bus about five.' When Timmy mentioned Guy the sound of his name brought panic, just as had her first glimpse of his home in the spring sunshine. Perhaps she had been crazy in the first place ever to have come here.

'Well, just as you like, of course.' Mrs Timpson gave in with remarkable good grace, not even attempting to get Celia to change her mind. Nor did she suggest that the gardener might run her back to Manchester as Celia had half expected she would.

Later, when Mrs Timpson rose to get tea, Celia realised that she hadn't once seemed inclined to discuss her decision to leave the shop and return to London. Perhaps, Celia concluded bitterly, like the others, she wasn't particularly interested.

Although Mrs Timpson had made hot scones and cream cakes for tea, Celia found she could scarcely eat them; her appetite, because of her surroundings, was almost non-existent. 'I really must go now,' she said hastily, declining another cup of tea as she jumped to her feet. 'If time waits for no man, neither do buses,' she smiled, with a kind of muddled flippancy.

'Yes, dear, I mean no. No, of course not . . .' Of a sudden Mrs Timpson looked flurried, as if she hadn't been paying a great deal of attention. 'If you would wait in the hall,' she went on, 'while I fetch my coat, I'll walk a little way with you. The doctor said some air would do me good.'

Celia slowly went into the hall where her own coat lay over a chair. The door of Guy's study, she saw, was half open, and unable to resist the temptation to have one last glimpse of a room which held so many memories, she walked quickly towards it. At the most she only had a minute.

It was empty, as she had known it would be, but she sensed immediately some aura about it, as if some faint essence of Guy's presence still lingered. Unwittingly she went over to the desk, running her fingers lovingly along the dark wood, thinking with painful longing of the dark head which she'd so often seen here.

'Were you looking for something, Celia?' A voice spoke deeply behind her, and she swung around in dismay to find Guy there, his face smoothly impassive as he surveyed the flushed wildness of her own.

'Guy!' For a long moment she was unable to add anything more. Through the frantic fluttering of her pulses she

183

could only stare at him, feeling a peculiar wave of faintness wash over her, just as it had done on that last day at the store. Only this time it seemed much worse. 'Guy ...' she tried again, and he caught hold of her swiftly as suddenly she knew no more.

When she came around she was lying on the sofa. Someone had switched on an electric fire and Guy was standing over her, a glass in his hand. Of Mrs Timpson there was no sign. 'I'm sorry,' she muttered, her voice weak, 'I must have been startled. I was just on my way ...'

'Will you shut up!' Guy cut her off tersely. 'Or if you can't do that, you could perhaps try telling me how I come to love a woman who chooses to faint at my feet?'

'I'm sorry,' she began, trying to evade the arm he was sliding around her, the proffered brandy. 'Guy!' she choked, her eyes wide on his grim face, the feeling of faintness back again, but for entirely different reasons. 'What did you say?'

He didn't answer, not right away. He ignored the beseeching expression in her wide-eyed gaze until she had taken a little of the brandy. 'You heard,' he said at last, studying the degree of colour returning to her pale cheeks.

'But,' she swallowed, her voice little more than a whisper, 'I don't understand.'

'Well, if words don't explain perhaps this should.' Slowly and deliberately he pulled her completely into his arms, and his mouth was on hers, bruising her soft lips until she stopped resisting him. Then they no longer hurt but were unbelievably gentle, exploring hers with an expertise of a man knowledgeable in the ways of women.

In that moment Celia knew she was lost for ever. He took possession not only of her lips but of her body too. She could scarcely breathe, she felt drugged, unable to think for herself, and her small hands tightened on his shoulders as something wild, almost primitive, was unleashed inside her. She heard herself moan as he rained kisses down on her face and neck and was helpless against the fire which was rapidly consuming her body.

'Guy!' she cried, as he lifted his mouth from hers, wanting only to cling to him as he held her gently from him.

'You love me too,' he said, no question in his short exultant statement, his eyes still dark with a depth of passion which might have frightened her once, but not now.

'Oh, yes,' she replied, her breath a sigh against his lips. 'The past two weeks have been terrible.'

'For me too,' he acknowledged thickly. 'I was coming back, Celia, I just couldn't stay away. I wanted to punish you for the things you said until I realised that hurt pride offered no kind of compensation for what I was losing. I was merely indulging in the same kind of weakness I'd so often imagined I saw in you. Ever since that first time I saw you all those years ago, a veritable little savage who slapped my astounded face, I've wanted you. It's too late now ever to let you escape.'

'I thought you loved Greta,' she said, 'and I thought she was attracted to you.'

'And you know what thought did, my darling!'

'You always seemed to dislike Lucy. I should never have said what I did, but I was distraught.'

'Celia ...' Frowning suddenly, Guy's eyes rested on her bewildered face. 'It was my concern for Lucy which perhaps gave that impression. You see, I tried to warn her for her own sake against Denis, but she would never listen.'

'But he's your cousin,' she protested.

'One so far removed that the relationship scarcely exists.'

'I don't understand——'

'Of course you don't,' Guy said softly, pulling her closer. 'I should have explained. Denis comes from a family of gamblers, potentially brilliant, and because there is this distant relationship I took a chance with him and gave him a job. In this he proved far from disappointing, only I didn't realise Lucy would get involved with him.'

'But he did like her?'

'I gather he liked her a lot,' Guy agreed dryly, 'until

Greta turned up. From the day he met her I'm afraid Lucy didn't have a chance, but it seems he kept her dangling as a sort of second string to his bow. If he couldn't have money he might settle for love.'

'That sounds cynical, and I still don't understand why he felt it necessary to run away,' persisted Celia.

'Probably he was afraid Greta might change her mind, or that her parents might change it for her. I gather they aren't at all enthusiastic about their new son-in-law, and, knowing this, Denis apparently was taking no risks.'

Celia still felt bewildered, although with Guy's arms possessively around her she had to force herself to concentrate. 'But surely, if Greta loved him——'

He regarded her gravely, his eyes wandering to her throbbing mouth. 'Young men like Denis, I've found, are often very insecure beneath all their surface bravado, but undoubtedly Greta's money will now provide the necessary prop. However, that's his problem, and just so long as Lucy isn't too badly hurt I suggest we forget about him. We have other things to talk about now that I've found you again.'

'How did you know I was here?' Celia heard herself asking. 'Was it simply coincidence?'

'No,' he smiled, his eyes glinting, 'Mrs Timpson told me when I rang this morning to ask how she was after her attack of influenza. I instructed her to keep you here until I arrived. As soon as she mentioned your name I knew I couldn't live another day without you. I've loved you far too long.'

'Yet you never came to London to find me,' she cried, finding it so difficult to believe him.

He said ruefully, 'I had to give you time, my darling. Time to grow up a little—to meet other men. You see, I'm thirty-six, so much older than you are. But who do you think was responsible for bringing you back? I'd kept a distant eye on you for three years and my patience was fast running out. Robin rang, begging you to come home, but I'm afraid it was I who indirectly put the thought into his head. It wasn't too difficult, and he had no idea I knew anything about his domestic problems.'

Celia lifted her head to look at him. There was so much she felt she ought to say, about Lucy and Greta, but all she could think of was how much she cared for this man who held her so gently. 'I thought I hated you, Guy,' she whispered, 'because you'd succeeded where my father failed. I know now, because Robin told me, that Father almost begged you to take the store off his hands when you didn't really want it. I also know that I love you, and if you can forgive me . . .'

Her voice trailed off, stopped by his kisses, his soft triumphant laughter as she melted in his embrace. 'Darling,' he teased gently, 'I'll forgive you anything if you promise to be my wife.'

She nodded, her eyes sapphire stars. 'If that's the worst of my punishments——' she began tremulously.

'Oh, no,' he threatened, drawing her closer, 'there'll be worse—after we're married!'

A few minutes later when Mrs Timpson knocked tentatively on the door, neither of them so much as heard her.

Send for your copy today!

The Harlequin Romance Catalog FREE!

Here's your chance to catch up on all the wonderful Harlequin Romance novels you may have missed because the books are no longer available at your favorite booksellers.

Complete the coupon and mail it to us. By return mail, we'll send you a copy of the latest Harlequin catalog. Then you'll be able to order the books you want directly from us.

Clip and mail coupon today.

Harlequin Reader Service
M.P.O. Box 707
Niagara Falls, N.Y. 14302

In Canada:
Harlequin Reader Service
Stratford, Ontario   N5A 6W4

Please send my FREE
Harlequin Romance Catalog!

NAME

ADDRESS

CITY

STATE }
PROV. }   ZIP }
                POSTAL CODE }   ROM 2112

Did you miss any of these exciting Harlequin Omnibus 3-in-1 volumes?

Anne Hampson #3
Heaven Is High (#1570)
Gold Is the Sunrise (#1595)
There Came a Tyrant (#1622)

Essie Summers #6
The House on Gregor's Brae (#1535)
South Island Stowaway (#1564)
A Touch of Magic (#1702)

Margaret Way #2
Summer Magic (#1571)
Ring of Jade (#1603)
Noonfire (#1687)

Margaret Malcolm #2
Marriage by Agreement (#1635)
The Faithful Rebel (#1664)
Sunshine on the Mountains (#1699)

Eleanor Farnes #2
A Castle in Spain (#1584)
The Valley of the Eagles (#1639)
A Serpent in Eden (#1662)

Kay Thorpe
Curtain Call (#1504)
Sawdust Season (#1583)
Olive Island (#1661)

18 magnificent Omnibus volumes to choose from:

Betty Neels #3
Tangled Autumn (#1569)
Wish with the Candles (#1593)
Victory for Victoria (#1625)

Violet Winspear

Violet Winspear #5
Raintree Valley (#1555)
Black Douglas (#1580)
The Pagan Island (#1616)

Anne Hampson

Anne Hampson #4
Isle of the Rainbows (#1646)
The Rebel Bride (#1672)
The Plantation Boss (#1678)

Margery Hilton
The Whispering Grove (#1501)
Dear Conquistador (#1610)
Frail Sanctuary (#1670)

Rachel Lindsay

Rachel Lindsay
Love and Lucy Granger (#1614)
Moonlight and Magic (#1648)
A Question of Marriage (#1667)

Jane Arbor

Jane Arbor #2
The Feathered Shaft (#1443)
Wildfire Quest (#1582)
The Flower on the Rock (#1665)

Great value in reading at $2.25 per volume

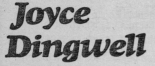

Joyce Dingwell #3
Red Ginger Blossom (#1633)
Wife to Sim (#1657)
The Pool of Pink Lilies (#1688)

Hilary Wilde

Hilary Wilde
The Golden Maze (#1624)
The Fire of Life (#1642)
The Impossible Dream (#1685)

Flora Kidd
If Love Be Love (#1640)
The Cave of the White Rose (#1663)
The Taming of Lisa (#1684)

Lucy Gillen

Lucy Gillen #2
Sweet Kate (#1649)
A Time Remembered (#1669)
Dangerous Stranger (#1683)

Gloria Bevan

Gloria Bevan
Beyond the Ranges (#1459)
Vineyard in a Valley (#1608)
The Frost and the Fire (#1682)

Jane Donnelly
The Mill in the Meadow (#1592)
A Stranger Came (#1660)
The Long Shadow (#1681)

Complete and mail this coupon today!

Mail coupon to:
Harlequin Books
MPO Box 707
Niagara Falls, N.Y. 14302

In Canada:
Harlequin Books
Stratford, Ont. N5A 6W4

Please send me the volumes indicated below. I am enclosing my check or money order for $2.25 for each volume ordered, plus 35¢ to cover postage and handling.

☐ Anne Hampson 3
☐ Essie Summers 6
☐ Margaret Way 2
☐ Margaret Malcolm 2
☐ Eleanor Farnes 2
☐ Kay Thorpe
☐ Betty Neels 3
☐ Violet Winspear 5
☐ Anne Hampson 4

☐ Margery Hilton
☐ Rachel Lindsay
☐ Jane Arbor 2
☐ Joyce Dingwell 3
☐ Hilary Wilde
☐ Flora Kidd
☐ Lucy Gillen 2
☐ Gloria Bevan
☐ Jane Donnelly

Number of volumes checked _____ @ $2.25 ea. = $ _____

N.Y. and N.J. residents add appropriate sales tax $_____

Postage and handling $ _____ .35

TOTAL $ _____

NAME _____
                        (please print)
ADDRESS _____

CITY _____

STATE/PROV. _____ ZIP/POSTAL CODE _____

ROM 2112